TROUBLE

WINTER SUN BOOK 3

ROE HORVAT

D1411820

Trouble

First edition
Published 2022 by Roe Horvat
Copyright © 2022 Roe Horvat
All rights reserved.

Edited by Karen Meeus, 2022.
Proofreading by Laura Williams, 2022.
Cover art by Roe Horvat, 2022.

❄

❄

Hugh has been in love with Kirby for years, which either makes him the most foolish or the most patient alpha on the planet. Because Kirby Matthews, the famous porn star and omega of everyone's wet dreams, is resolutely single. But Hugh knows the real Kirby underneath the armor of glamour and snark. When an opportunity arises to be with him during heat, Hugh will do whatever it takes—even get naked in front of the cameras.

Kirby has made it big time, from homelessness to international stardom. He can now enjoy the small things like the feeling of silk on his skin, long showers, and cupcakes. Life is comfortingly simple. But then his long-time crush auditions for a role in his next film, and Kirby is torn. Getting entangled with a close friend, a member of his makeshift family, is a certifiably stupid idea. But saying no to Hugh? Beefy arms, shaved head, and growly voice— all rough alpha, but with a ridiculously soft heart... How is Kirby supposed to resist such temptation?

The most anticipated porn flick of the year, starring Kirby Matthews in heat. Ten days on set, with no privacy and no space to explore their feelings. You can't fall in love while filming porn, right?

Trouble is an omegaverse erotic romance featuring high heat, friends to lovers, hurt/comfort. HEA, standalone.

ACKNOWLEDGMENTS

As always, a heartfelt thank-you to Karen, Laura, and Vin, for their excellence and endless patience.

I'm grateful to my dear patrons for reading early versions of this story, loving it, and making it better.

I owe my deepest gratitude to every kind, generous person who invested their energy into reading my drafts and advanced review copies, and who listened to my whines with empathy. Each and every one of you who reads, writes, publishes, promotes, and supports LGBTQ+ stories, thank you.

CONTENT WARNING

The novel is an omegaverse, non-shifter, paranormal romance, with the possibility of male pregnancy.

Potential triggers
Abuse and homelessness off-page, retold as a character's memories.

For adult readers only.

PROLOGUE

HUGH

I stumbled to the kitchen on unsteady legs, half of my brain still asleep. My nephew, Monty, sat at the table, already dressed for school. He was a good kid, but he didn't get that from me. My little brother Jay had been the nice boy in our family, and I used to be a menace. Until life taught me to shut up and work or else.

"Hey, little dude."

"Hi."

I ruffled Monty's hair, and he squirmed, ducking away.

"Where's your dad?"

"Gone. You've overslept."

"No, I haven't. We still have fifteen minutes before we must leave."

"We were almost late last week."

"Almost. We're *never* late."

I poured myself the last of the coffee Jay must have made and sat down in front of the opulent selection of different cereal boxes. We didn't have money to splurge in this household, but Monty was skinny like a stick figure and picky as hell. Cereal with whole milk for breakfast was an easy way to get the calories into him.

"Shovel on, boy. A long day awaits."

"Dad says you're not going to the park with us tomorrow."

"I'm sorry, Monty. I can't. My boss's getting married, so I'll be at the wedding."

"And we can't come?"

"I didn't ask. It's until late, and there won't be any kids your age, so I thought you'd find it boring. But I'll bring you cake."

"Cool. Will you be drinking alcohol?"

I bit my lip. My nephew was growing up so fast I got dizzy watching him. "I think so. Some adults do that at weddings."

"Mr. Donovan says alcohol is poison."

"For little kids like you, definitely. Who's Mr. Donovan?"

"Lenny's dad. Lenny says he works for God."

"It's called a preacher. Your cereal's getting soggy, monkey."

Monty dutifully scooped up another spoonful. "And will Kirby be there?" he asked with his mouth full.

"Why do you ask?"

"I heard you and Dad. Dad said you like him like a boyfriend."

When did the little spy hear that?

"Um. I'm pretty sure we didn't say anything like that."

"Dad said you've got it bad."

"He meant I have a bad rash on my back. It itches like hell. Will you scratch it for me?"

"Eww. You're disgusting, Uncle Hughie."

Since he'd started first grade, Monty insisted on calling me just Hugh because Uncle Hughie was for little kids, but sometimes he slipped. I found it adorable.

"Do you want some more? Cinnamon crunch?"

"No. Thanks."

"Okay. Go brush your teeth. Quick!"

After I dropped Monty off at school, I went to the gym. My shift at the pub started at three, so I had time to go home for a quick nap before that. Going to bed at two and getting up at seven thirty was rough, especially before another evening behind the bar. Luckily, I only had to do it on Thursday nights.

Jay was a nurse, and since he'd had Monty, he worked mornings at a local GP clinic, seven to half past three. He got paid less than if he did night shifts at a hospital, but it allowed him to be with Monty on afternoons. We'd had this setup for years; Jay got ready for work, left breakfast on the kitchen table, and woke Monty up just as he was leaving. I got Monty ready for school, dropped him off, ran errands, hunted for groceries, cleaned the apartment or did laundry, and then I went to work. Jay picked Monty up in the afternoons on his way from the clinic. With our new schedule at Burke's and my recent promotion to floor manager, I worked Monday to Saturday from three to eleven thirty or five to two in the morning. When I came home, Jay was usually passed out cold.

We got tired, but we ran our home like a well-oiled machine. The only downside was that Jay and I only saw each other for a few hours over the weekends, which we spent talking about family logistics and money.

Always the fucking money.

We would have done okay if it weren't for the debt. The interest payments ate twenty percent of our income while the loan remained nearly the same. I had a plan to get us out of the deadlock, but I needed a small capital. I couldn't save and couldn't get another loan because I was barely paying off the first one. So yes, my life was all about money —the constant lack of it.

My phone rang just as I was putting away the barbells.

"Hi, Jay. Everything okay?"

"Lunch break. Yes. I forgot to leave you a message yesterday, but the guy from the bank called. We don't qualify for the loan deferment."

Fuck.

I closed my eyes and took a deep breath. "Okay. We knew this would happen, right?"

"Yeah."

"We'll manage."

"I know. I'm so sorry."

"I'm sorry too, Jaybird. We're in this together."

"Lunch on Sunday?"

"Yes. I'll be at home. I promised Monty I'll bring cake from the wedding."

"Okay. Just don't let me eat more than one piece, okay? I need this figure so I can find myself a sugar daddy."

I chuckled. "If you actually went out to meet people, you'd have plenty of those, hot stuff."

"Unless Burke suddenly starts bring-your-kid-to-work Fridays at the pub, that's a moot point."

"We need a sitter. I'll ask around."

"We're not doing this now," Jay said wearily. We'd had this argument before.

"It was you who said you wanted a sugar daddy."

"And I'm already regretting it. I need to go back to work."

"Go. Love you, Jaybird. See you tomorrow."

"You'll be home and awake?"

"For a few hours. The ceremony starts at four. The party is at six at the pub."

"Will Kirby be there?" Jay teased.

"Fuck off, little brother. Anyway. I'll need to sleep in, but I'll see you and Monty for lunch."

"Great. See you then."

"Bye."

I slipped my phone into my pocket and groaned. I should make more of an effort to help Jay date. I couldn't remember the last time he went out with someone. Two or three years ago? My little brother was cute and smart. Although, I wasn't sure I'd approve of anyone for Jay and Monty. They needed someone kind, reliable, and protective. The only alpha like that I knew was getting married tomorrow.

IT WAS RARE, but sometimes it happened, right? I wasn't crazy, and I sure wasn't the only one. Sometimes, people just clicked. A few minutes of casual chatting, a fleeting touch, a deep breath pulling in his scent, and you knew.

When I first talked to Kirby Matthews, I knew within ten minutes. He was my omega. My dream boy. Except life sucked, nothing ever came easy, and we both had more baggage than an airport terminal during the holiday season.

Maybe I was a fool to fall in love with him. Or maybe I had to be patient.

Today, Kirby looked especially lovely. The extra effort he'd put into his outfit for his best friend's wedding made him look softer around the edges than his usual unapproachable bad-boy persona. His long legs were encased in tight slacks, and a white shirt hugged his torso. His thick, almost black hair curled and fell over his forehead in an artful mess, and when he noticed me staring, he smirked briefly, full lips glistening with gloss, cheeks a bit flushed. His dark gaze flicked around restlessly like he wasn't sure if he should be on his guard or not.

"I don't like the concept of weddings," he said. "I mean, I'm happy for Em. But it seems like such a hassle, and you must feed all these people."

"Burke and Emerson have friends and family they want to celebrate with. I think it's nice."

A shadow passed over Kirby's boyish features, his catlike eyes narrowing slightly. "Emerson doesn't have a family."

"Aren't you like his family?"

He flashed me a sweet smile, too brief to be entirely honest. "I am." Then he wrinkled his nose, scanning the crowd. "Sort of. Anyway. They love each other. I get it. But it's not like a piece of paper and a party will help them to uphold that."

"Look at them."

The song morphed into something slower, and Burke hoisted Emerson up, holding the small omega easily by a firm grip under his thighs. Laughing, Emerson wrapped his arms around Burke's neck. His expression turned serious, and he leaned in to plant a long, tender kiss on Burke's mouth. Burke closed his eyes, swaying his now husband from side to side to the rhythm. They were positively glowing.

Kirby made a noise next to me. He sort of groaned, but it wasn't with displeasure. He seemed uncomfortable and a little confused. If I didn't know better, I'd think he looked lost.

"What's really bugging you, Kirby?"

Scratching his neck, Kirby glanced at me and sighed.

"I'm being a bitch, aren't I? I'm happy for Emerson. I really am."

"I know."

I waited him out. He'd tell me if he wanted to.

"He's like my little brother, and now he's all grown up and moving on with his life. Starting his own family. I think I'll just miss him. That's all."

"You're moving on as well."

At that, Kirby gifted me with his rare sardonic laughter. "Oh yes, you bet! I have a new project." He waggled his eyebrows. "My first heat porn, and the director is an omega. I haven't met him yet, but it sounds different. Allegedly, he's chosen me specifically."

The idea of Kirby in heat, cameras around, his body glowing with sweat... *Yeah.* "An omega, huh? It's not common in the industry, is it?"

"No, it's not. I'm curious about him. I'm supposed to meet him on Tuesday. Also, the pay is like five times as much as I usually get, plus a percentage if the movie does well. And if they really pay me. I'm still wondering if I'm being conned."

"Have you checked up on him?"

"Yeah. He seems legit. Did a few artsy erotic flicks even, not just plain porn. If it works out, the price tag on my ass will go up." He smacked his lips and gulped down the last of his drink. "And I just heard myself say a bunch of 'ifs' in a row. Can we get another one?"

"Sure. What do you want?"

"GT? Oh, and one of those little cupcakes that are on the bar. Chocolate, please."

"I'll be right back."

Burke had hired catering staff so none of his regular employees had to work at his wedding. He was a nice guy, through and through. I ordered from the open bar and watched Kirby as I waited for our drinks.

He slouched on the bench in the corner booth, the unbuttoned shirt revealing a triangle of tanned skin. He picked at the fabric of the seat with his long fingers. A man approached him, an alpha around forty, and Kirby said something, smiling up at the guy. The alpha strode away fast, and Kirby rolled his eyes.

Kirby wasn't super famous or anything. *Yet*. Because with his face and body, with his sharp mind and hell, the way he moved, he was bound to make it big one day soon. He did get recognized sometimes, which was what I guessed had happened with that man. Some people assumed that because Kirby did porn, he was almost like public property. Random guys hit on him all the time, and he either politely declined or got gloriously bitchy when they persisted. It was fun to watch.

There were these moments, little fragments, when I almost believed he felt the same about me as I did about him. Like now. After Kirby blew off the other guy and saw me walking back to him with two GTs in one hand and a cupcake in the other, his features rearranged from annoyance into an excited grin. The tip of his tongue peeked out again as he smiled at me, and he relaxed deeper into the corner seat the closer I came, like he couldn't wait for me to join him again. It could have been the cupcake I was carrying, though.

"Thank you, kind sir," he drawled and took the cupcake

from me. He shoved half of it into his mouth and reached for the drink.

"Fu-in' dee-licioupf," he mumbled around the food, and I had to laugh. Kirby was bordering on skinny, but Lord, did he love to eat.

I sat next to him and clinked his glass. The bartender had overdone it with the ice, but I wouldn't complain. Free horse and all that.

"Did that guy bother you?"

"Who?"

I tilted my chin in the direction the alpha had left.

"Oh, that one." Kirby smirked. "I think I handled it quite nicely."

"How?"

"He complimented me on my ass, which he seemed to remember in detail from my films. Then he asked if he could get me a drink. He didn't seem to hear me when I said no. So I told him I'd just sucked the bartender's huge dick under the counter. Hence my drinks and ass are taken care of tonight."

With some effort, I managed to force the GT down without spluttering.

"How rude of you!" I cried with outrage. Kirby knew me well enough to know I was joking. "This is a wedding celebration, Mr. Matthews. What if the man's someone's uncle?"

"Someone's creepy uncle?" Kirby batted his eyelashes at me. "I'm so sorry. Should I go apologize? Maybe suck him off too so he doesn't feel left out?" He popped the rest of the cupcake into his mouth.

I chuckled. "I shouldn't leave you unattended."

"I agree. Keep the creeps away, please." He wiggled closer to me, and I threw my arm around his shoulders.

After demolishing the cupcake, Kirby took a few large gulps, downing the entire cooler, so I mimicked him.

"Dance with me?" he asked.

"Sure."

I could feel the alcohol doing its job, my blood warming up. Wrapping my arms around Kirby's slender frame, I exhaled. He was tall for an omega, just the right height for his hair to tickle my nose. His skin felt cool through the thin shirt.

"Mmm, you're so nice and warm, Hughie." His soft giggle made me wonder how many drinks he'd had. I was already buzzing, but he might have managed even more than me.

"Oh yeah, I'm the hot stuff."

"If the winter gets nasty like last year, I could borrow you as my personal heater."

"Kitten, I'll warm your bed anytime. Just say the word."

"Kitten? That's new."

"It's your eyes." I leaned in and whispered into his ear, "And claws."

Kirby laughed. "You're supposed to keep the creeps away, not get creepy yourself, remember?"

It was a game we played. We'd flirt and joke, but it never went anywhere. Kirby would always put on the brakes before it could get weird. I couldn't get a read on him. Was it because he wasn't interested, or did he have some strict don't-shit-where-you-eat rule? Since Burke and Emerson had gotten together, we saw each other at least once a week, and I liked to think that the pub had become sort of a safe haven for Kirby. So maybe he didn't want to mess that up by sleeping with the staff.

Except tonight, he seemed to have let his guard down. The song went on about second chances and undying love, and Kirby got pliant in my embrace, our bodies moving in sync.

It didn't seem out of place to nuzzle his hairline—only a fleeting brush. His scent always grabbed me by my balls. Maybe tonight would be the night? For once, there wasn't a bar counter between us. My grand opportunity to charm my boy, catch him, and keep him.

Kirby leaned back and scanned my face. His dark eyes were glassy but still perfectly focused. He ran his fingers along my neck, nails scratching through my short hair, and I shivered.

"You know, Hugh, you're such a deadly combination of sexy and sweet. Like *deadly*."

Oh please, let this be the night. "I thought you were immune?"

He cocked his head to the side and snorted like I was being stupid. "With these shoulders"—he squeezed said muscles—"the tats and the stubble." He ran his fingers along my jaw. "And those cute puppy eyes." Holding my gaze, he licked his lips. "I could throw you on the floor and ride you like a fucking rocket all the way to sunrise." His laughter rang around us while my belly swooped and my dick hardened. He didn't feel it with the breath of space between our bodies. "Deadly sexy." His voice got husky.

Yeah, he must be drunk.

"Like I've told you several times, Kirby. You only have to say the word, and I'll be on my knees with my mouth around your dick, ready to obey any command you give me."

"Ha. I highly doubt that. No way are *you* the least bit subby."

"Usually not. But for you, I'd kneel in a heartbeat."

Kirby paused, frowning up at me. The crease between

his eyebrows was so cute I had to bite my lip to stop my sudden urge to kiss the spot.

"You really mean that, don't you?" he asked.

"I've always wanted you. You know that."

He clicked his tongue. "This is such a stupid, dumbass idea."

Despite his harsh words, he leaned into my embrace, and we resumed dancing. Truth be told, we more like swayed in place, my hands on his hips. He kept one arm around my shoulder and patted the center of my chest.

"You're drunk too. Your ears get red when you've had one too many."

"A little bit. You know me too well. It's not fair."

"Life's not fair, Hugh." Kirby looked around, scanning the crowd. It was a reflex of his, always being aware of his surroundings, always alert, ready to bolt or fight. Except here at Burke's Pub, closed for a private event, he was as safe as he could get. Even if Burke let some assholes cause trouble, which no one dared, I wouldn't let anyone bother Kirby.

"I just want to dance some more," he said.

I tugged him closer, and he went willingly, laying his head on my shoulder. I inhaled the scent of his hair, remnants of coconut shampoo and my Kirby. Well...technically not mine. But maybe one day.

"You're cuddly today. I like that." I kissed his forehead. Apparently, I was in a self-destructive mood today.

"I don't get to cuddle often."

"You know where to find me." I tightened my hold on him. Another slow song rose in volume, and we shuffled from foot to foot. "Kirby."

"Mm?"

"Remind me why we're not together."

He chuckled, sounding a bit exasperated. "Because I don't fuck people I don't work with. And because you're my friend. We've been over this."

"You only fuck people who do porn?"

"Damn, you *are* drunk."

"Only a little. I will remember everything tomorrow."

"I'll call you and quiz you."

"Please, do."

Why did he have to smell so good? "Kirby."

"What now?"

"So if I did porn too, would you have sex with me?"

Kirby chuckled, shaking in my arms. "Sure, Hugh. If you were a porn star, I'd fuck your brains out."

"Cool."

"You're hard," he murmured, his voice barely audible above the music.

"You too."

"It's nice. Just hold me."

We danced for ages, my erection tingling against Kirby's stomach, and I could feel his hard cock at the top of my thigh. We clung to each other, slowly swaying our hips, and the yearning got almost painful. My dick seemed to have developed its own heartbeat with the way it throbbed. For a second, Kirby pressed against me harder, a move almost like a thrust, and we both groaned.

Abruptly, he pushed away.

"Can we go out? I need to breathe."

"Sure."

He hugged my arm, staying close while we ambled through the thinning crowd outside onto the street. I had no idea what time it was, but the city seemed deserted. Maybe sometime after two in the morning? Kirby stepped back into my arms, so I just went with it. Maybe he was cuddly because he was afraid to be alone. He might have felt that Emerson was leaving him behind. Maybe seeing all the love and togetherness made him feel sad. It made me sad a little, too. Whatever the reason, I took it and was grateful. In my slightly inebriated state, I didn't worry about the possible consequences as much as I might have done otherwise.

Kirby shuddered and heaved a sigh.

"You're cold."

"I'm good. You're emanating heat."

I ran my hands up and down his back, and he wiggled, making a cute noise of contentment. My erection hadn't gone down in the slightest, but the cold air helped to clear my head.

He grinned up at me, the tip of his tongue peeking out between his teeth. I both loved and hated when he did that. It made me want to bite him.

"Do you act like my friend only to get into my pants?" Kirby blurted the question like it was something that had bothered him for some time.

"I do want to get into your pants, yes. I also want to get to know you better, make love to you, and spend more time with you."

"People like me don't *make love*." The way he said it, with a slight tremor in his voice and not even a hint of his usual sarcasm...

I cupped his jaw, his soft, thin stubble tickling my palm. "We could."

He blinked a couple of times. "I really want to kiss you."

I was going to regret this once he bailed on me again. But if I didn't kiss him, I'd regret it even more.

Knowing he could escape me at any moment, I bent down and captured his upper lip between mine.

Holy fucking insanity.

It was like the pull of two magnets—when they get so close, they just snap together and you can't pry them apart. We both struggled to shove our tongue into the other's mouth until we found a rhythm, and Lord, the taste of him had my cock dripping precum.

"Fuck, Hugh."

"I know. More."

"Oh yes, we definitely need more of that."

I grabbed his ass cheeks and squeezed them as I dove back into his mouth. He sucked on my tongue, humming, then angled his head so I could lick deeper. He moaned when I mimicked a slow fucking motion with my tongue, rubbing it against the roof of his mouth.

"Can we go to your place?" he whispered against my wet lips.

"We can't. I don't live alone."

"Ugh. Don't tell me you're one of those—"

"Not what you think," I hurried to explain. "My younger brother and his kid are staying with me for the time being."

"Oh."

"Can we go to yours?"

"One bedroom. My roommate's at home."

"You taste like sin." I nipped at his lip, but he leaned away.

"Fucking hell, Hugh. What are we doing?"

"I want you so much."

"I want you too, for fuck's sake. Always have. But I'm not having sex with you in the alley behind Burke's Pub. I'm not having sex in any alleys anymore. Never again."

I rested my forehead against his, trying to calm the fuck down. What was the right thing to say? *I've been in love with*

you for months. I'm burning up here. Let's just...go get a hotel?
And then what?

"We shouldn't be doing this anyway," he said. "It's for the best, isn't it?"

"No. We totally should be doing this."

"I'm sorry. It's been a bad idea."

"Why?"

"You're one of the nicest people in my life, Hugh."

"Don't friend-zone me. Please, Kirby."

He searched my gaze, and I could literally see him sobering up by the second. My moment was gone. He'd escaped me again, just like always, dammit. "You're completely, absolutely, irresistibly lovely all around, Hugh."

"Kirby, please, we can—"

Putting a finger over my lips, he shook his head. "The cold and the sexual frustration help me think."

"Don't think. Please, don't think," I mumbled against his lips. "Just kiss me some more."

He groaned and buried his face at the base of my throat. "Argh! Dammit, Hugh! Shit, fuck, pissload of shitfuck!"

Not knowing what else to do, I combed my fingers through his hair. Pissload of shitfuck was about right.

It took a long while for him to speak again. Feeling the doom and gloom seep into us both, I waited. When he finally opened his mouth, I wasn't surprised, just really fucking sad.

"I don't want to lose you over a drunken hookup." He lifted his head, and his eyes didn't have the same glassy film over them as they did just a few minutes ago. "Let's stay in each other's lives."

"As friends." I couldn't help but sound defeated.

"Yeah. I have only a few of those. Please, don't give up

on me after this. I'm sorry. I didn't mean to lead you on, I swear. I don't know what got into me. I normally have myself under control, but..."

"Shh. It's okay." I did understand. I hated it, but I did understand.

He kissed my cheek. "Hughie."

I grabbed him and squeezed him to me, swallowing against the lump in my throat.

"Fuck, Kirby, you're trouble."

"Exactly my point."

I nestled one last kiss into his hair and inhaled deeply. The devil knew when he would let me touch him again.

KIRBY

This was what I would become famous for.

When I'd agreed to this gig, I thought it would be like the last flick I'd done, except with another director and with a small added bonus—I'd be in heat. Contraception was provided and paid for—they'd already inserted the small device into my womb, and according to the doctor, it was more than ninety-nine percent effective. It had occurred to me at the swanky doctor's office that this movie might be better funded, but I didn't think much about it. I wasn't used to being optimistic.

The first day I met the director, I realized I was in for something different. First and foremost, he was an omega. In the porn industry, the omegas were almost always the guys in front of the camera and not the ones behind it. And second, he looked all posh and smooth like a politician or a businessman. He even had a suit on when we met. The last director I'd worked with met me dressed in jeans, a torn sleeveless shirt, and a backward ballcap. This guy, Brian was his name, was all sleek and cool, from the tips of his styled hair to his gleaming dress shoes. He shook my hand, offered me coffee, and asked if I'd read the fine print before I signed the contract.

"Yes, sir. The only thing that stood out to me was the doctor's exam afterward. Why do I need that?" I really hoped they didn't secretly plan on something creepy or dangerous. I had my fantasies, but I didn't do hardcore kink. I didn't trust anyone enough.

"Oh, that. We merely want to make sure that you're not pregnant. The contraceptive you've been given should be one of the safest on the market, but we're not taking any chances. In case you, against all odds, get pregnant, this way you'll know as soon as possible. The compensation will be paid out—forty percent immediately and the remaining sixty after the child is born if you decide to carry to term."

The compensation was fifty thousand. I had to recount the zeroes and almost swallowed my tongue. Fifty thousand dollars. For a while there, I hoped I'd get knocked up, but the chance was basically nil.

"How do you feel?" Brian smiled at me. He looked like someone's dad and not a porn director. Did he have kids?

"Um. Kinda excited, to be honest."

He grinned wider. "Wonderful. You've met your colleagues already. What's your impression?"

"Great." What was I supposed to say? Four alphas. All of them fucking underwear models. I hadn't seen their dicks, but this was porn so I could imagine. My hands were clammy. "Sorry to be blunt, but why me? I'm a former rent boy and did only some low-budget movies during the past year. It's not like I have a name or anything." And I'd seen the other guys at the audition last month. Holy shit. Some of those boys were beautiful.

Brian squinted at me. "I saw those movies, yes. See, Kirby, you have something that's very rare in this industry."

I raised my eyebrows at him.

"Visible enjoyment. You look like you're having the time of your life when you're having sex on camera." He shrugged. "You can also be subtle and changeable. You have a talent."

I had a talent for getting fucked. Well, I'd take it and be grateful because having a stable income and a place to stay still hadn't lost its charm. Besides, getting those four porn stars for the duration of the heat would be the experience of a lifetime.

"I want you to meet our consultant. Come with me."

A consultant? Did he mean someone to take care of the payouts and taxes and such? Why would I need to meet him? We passed another office and ended up in a room with low sofas and a coffee maker. A man sat there doing something on his phone, and he looked nothing like a tax consultant.

"Walter, this is Kirby."

The guy shot up and turned to me. He was about forty, a tall alpha with a sly, somewhat cocky smirk, dressed in black jeans with holes on the knees and a leather jacket. His face made me apprehensive for no specific reason.

"Kirby, this is Walter Sébastien. He's a former heat teacher, and he'll be present for a large part of the production. Besides your co-stars, he'll be the only alpha on the set. He'll make sure that we do things right."

The man shook my hand and smiled toothily. A former heat teacher? Meaning he used to guide rich single omegas through their heats. If he was an omega, he'd be a rent boy. A whore. But alphas who fucked for money were "healers" and "teachers." Yeah, right. I swallowed my bitterness. I guessed he must have had a bunch of training and certifications, so it wasn't entirely the same thing, and I should be glad there'd be a sort-of supervisor present. Walter Sébastien looked all excited about the prospect of watching me get gang-banged during heat.

"Um. Do things right?" I checked. "What do you mean by that?"

Brian smiled and hugged my shoulders as if we were old friends.

"See, Kirby, since the beginning, the porn industry has been focused on alphas, on their viewing enjoyment and their needs. In recent years, we've seen a shift. More creators are releasing content that pays tribute to omega pleasure. It gets even more distinct with the surplus of amateur footage getting shared each day." He paused dramatically, and I could tell he really dug his own shit. I didn't mind. Whatever got me a decent job and a paycheck, I was in. "What I want to do is take this one step further. I want to show a genuine heat experience with maximum pleasure for the omega. While there's an abundance of heat porn made all the time, within mainstream production, the omega never transcends his confines as a mere object of the alpha's desire. He's a crude fantasy without substance, a wet hole for the knot. I want to make a movie that omegas can identify with, that reflects their own desires and fulfills their fantasies. I want omegas to watch it and immerse themselves in pleasure. They'll wish to become you."

I thought I got what he was saying, but he sounded a bit too fancy for my taste, which made me suspicious. It was just fucking, after all.

"What Brian is trying to say is that we'll make sure our boys keep blowing your mind. They're not here to get off on you. They're here to get you off."

I smirked. I might like Walter Sébastien after all.

FUNNY THING, I was supposed to sleep on set. The heat waves could be quite unpredictable and come whenever. The deal was that while the alphas could go rest from time to time in a separate bedroom nearby, I was to stay here.

So after the first day of filming—which had been just me stuffing myself with a nice big dildo on the evening before the heat—an assistant handed me a bathrobe and showed me to the bathroom. I showered, and when I came back, the equipment was turned off and shoved to the sides, and the bedroom looked almost normal. Brian sat in an armchair in front of a tray of food.

"Hope this is okay."

I eyed the tray. It was only healthy stuff. Soup, salad, some expensive bread with seeds in it, and a glass of juice. I wasn't too hungry—my appetite always disappeared close to heat—so it was fine.

"Sure. Thank you."

"Good." He clasped his hands together and rubbed them. "I'll let you sleep soon. The crew is staying on this floor. Once you feel a wave approaching, push the red button here." He pointed at a small panic button by the bed. "I don't care if it's at four in the morning. The sooner you let me know, the better. After the first wave, someone will be here with you all the time."

"Okay." He was looking at me like he wanted to say something more, so I waited.

"Are you feeling good?" he asked.

"Yeah. I'm glad we did the dildo scene first. Made me nice and relaxed." I winked. I actually preferred making solo stuff, but Brian didn't need to know that.

"You were wonderful. We have excellent footage from today."

"Cool. Thanks." I dug into the salad.

Brian wasn't finished, though. "You've had several sessions with Walter," he said slowly, eyeing me curiously.

Walter was supposed to prepare me and the alphas for the filming. Safety, sexual preferences, hard limits, things about my heat—stuff like that. But we'd stumbled upon some old shit when we'd talked, and one thing had led to another... In the end, Walter had picked my brain for hours because he thought I'd had "traumatic experiences." *Well, duh.* However, he didn't blab to Brian about the specifics because he kind of became my sex therapist and was bound by confidentiality.

"Walter was great. Thanks for that."

Brian nodded, but his eyes wandered around. "Look. Um. You've been through things I can't even imagine. And... In an ideal world, I would wish to make this a positive and maybe even cathartic experience for you."

"Walter identified my triggers, and the guys will respect my limits," I said. "We're good."

Sighing, Brian scratched his neck and blew out a breath. "We both know that this industry causes harm to people on a daily basis. I work hard to create stuff that's different." He looked me in the eye, all sad and worried, and I realized that Brian genuinely cared. That it wasn't just talk. "I want to create erotic content that's liberating for omegas. I would be the worst hypocrite if I hurt one of my performers in the process. Do you get what I mean?"

"I think so."

"I need you to feel safe, okay? So if something's not right, tell me. If you're afraid, feel threatened, forced, uncomfortable, or just want a different ice cream flavor, tell me. Immediately. And I will fix it."

Not like he could fix *me*. But he was trying, and I appreciated it.

"Brian, you brought in Walter, and you've chosen great guys for me to work with. We're good. I'm actually looking forward to it."

Finally, he seemed to relax. "Okay. Good."

I tried the soup, and it was so delicious I suddenly felt hungry, heat or no heat. "Soup's fantastic, thanks."

Brian patted my back and watched me eat for a while. He wasn't creepy about it, so I didn't mind.

"You like food, don't you?"

I grinned, tapping the spoon on my lips. "What tipped you off? The piggy noises I make?"

He laughed and stood. "Good night, Kirby. And thank you for today."

"No problem."

After I'd eaten, I went to brush my teeth and pee. I worried I wouldn't be able to sleep with the shadows of the equipment looming in the corners and the strange sounds of the studio. But I must have fallen asleep almost immediately.

NOW THIS WAS as close to nirvana as anyone had ever gotten. I barely had to move because the alpha under me, Dex was his name, lifted me up and down on his cock. Dex was fucking gorgeous. A tall black guy with an eight-pack, smoldering eyes, and the cheekbones of a god. And damn, what a cock. It was, no contest, the greatest dick I'd ever gotten into me. Maybe it was the heat, but shit, I loved that dick. Right now, it stroked the front wall of my hole and grazed the mouth to my womb on each thrust. I was coming again. Or maybe I was coming still. Who cared?

Eric held my head with both hands, thrusting into my mouth. His cock was shorter than Dex's but fat and delicious. The taste of his precum made me groan. There was so much of it that it leaked into my mouth. Eric liked me—I could tell. He kept petting my hair and touching my face when he fucked my mouth, and he stared at me with this intense look in his eyes. Yeah, he liked me.

My entire torso was covered in cum. Mine, Claude's, and Max's. I felt filthy and fucking awesome. Claude and Max were rubbing their swollen dicks on me where they could. From what I'd heard, having a knot grow outside of an omega's body could be unpleasant. But Brian said the exposed knots were part of the plan. They "exhibited the erotic power of the omega." Brian said shit like that on a regular basis.

The best moment was yet to come. This had been Walter's idea, and I was so in.

Claude and Max took my nipples into their mouths. The way they sucked was bordering on painful and absolutely fucking perfect. They opened their mouths wide, took the fleshy parts in, and pulled while rubbing the undersides with their tongues. The twin sensations were overwhelming. I couldn't help the keening sounds I kept making around Eric's cock. Suddenly, Eric retreated. He stroked himself with both hands while his knot grew. A fucking gallon of cum landed in my mouth and across my sweaty face. The taste was amazing. I gulped it all down, grabbed the knot, and licked all around the swollen cock.

"Great, Kirby! Keep going."

As if I could tear myself away. I made love to that thing, cleaning it, kissing, suckling. Eric stroked my hair, looking at me as if I was about to push out his firstborn. The guy was sweet. Then the suction on my nipples tightened, Dex shoved his cock deeper into me, and I lost coordination. I pulled Eric's knot to my face, holding it close, while I came my brains out for the hundredth time. And still, they kept sucking. I was going to start making milk if they kept it up.

Strange sensations gathered in my torso. From the pulling on my nipples, small electric sparkles arose, tendrils of energy shooting outward, and my entire chest throbbed, the muscles underneath my nipples all warm. The feeling was nothing but exquisite. I threw my head back and wailed. Eric's knot rubbed over my open lips.

I pushed my chest out, chasing the amazing suction.

"That's it, guys. Just a bit longer." It was Walter's voice. "He's almost there."

Where? Was there more?

My nipples felt electric already. They prickled, and the flesh underneath them began tingling. More. And even more. *Oh fuck!*

"Fuuuck! Fuuuuuck!" I screamed.

And then I exploded. The tingles became fireworks.

"Dex, now." Again, Walter. But I barely understood what was happening.

My nipples fucking climaxed. That was how it felt. Every sucking pull sent waves of pleasure outward, drowning my entire body in it. Dex's cock thrust even harder, his hands squeezed my hips, and another explosion of pleasure tore through me, this time from my very center. He'd breached the channel to my womb.

A small frisson of fear made my eyes go wide. I couldn't

take more. They'd fry my brain. But then the sensations in my nipples met and tangled with the tendrils coming from my womb, and...yeah. There really wasn't a way to describe that feeling. Dex doused my womb with cum, Claude and Max sucked my chest, Eric pushed his knot into my mouth, and I went to heaven.

ONCE I'D SLEPT it off, knotted and wrapped in Dex's arms, Brian showed me a few clips.

It looked like a sacred ritual or something. The four massive alphas surrounded my pale, slim body, hitting all my sweet spots all at once.

I got wet watching the moment Eric came on my face and into my mouth. The way I gazed up at him and then grabbed his knot...well, shit. I looked like a greedy animal, and it was hot.

The detail of my groin with Dex's knot growing in me blew my mind. I could see how my underbelly bulged a little with the knotting, but what was fascinating was when the camera zoomed in on my reddened dick. It fucking danced. Untouched and exposed, my erection throbbed and jerked, spitting small pearls of cum all over the place like a tiny fountain. My balls contracted with the breeding orgasm that I would forever remember as the most insane rush of my entire life.

I got now what Brian meant by showcasing omega pleasure.

I didn't remember much of the aftermath, so it was interesting to see it on screen. My chest was blotched with red, drops of cum everywhere. Claude and Max kissed and licked the tips of my nipples. I watched, mesmerized, as the me on the screen pulled on Eric's hips. I held him close, rubbing my face against his knot like a cat. Had I really done that? Wow. Apparently. Max crawled down my body and began licking my cock. It flexed under his tongue. Dex circled his hips, and my body went limp. He must have pulled out of my womb. I seemed out of it. Then the three big burly alphas cleaned me all over. They kissed and licked, wiped with washcloths, while their exposed knots brushed my skin here and there. All the time, Dex rocked my knotted body. My eyes were closed, but my cock was still hard, and sometimes it jerked. I must have still been buzzing. Finally, the three alphas stepped away, climbing off the bed. Dex curled around me, and the light dimmed.

Brian squeezed my shoulders. "This is going to be groundbreaking, Kirby."

AND BRIAN HAD BEEN RIGHT.

A year and a half had gone by since I'd made it big. We'd won awards, and I'd gotten more money than I'd ever dreamed of. The movie became the most watched porn flick in a decade. There were accolades, and there was criticism of course, shaming, and plenty of hate mail. But I was too happy to give the noise much attention.

For the first time in my life I had my own place, an entire freaking apartment. Two bedrooms in a high-rise in an okay part of Dalton City and a parking spot in an underground garage that I'd never use.

Sex toy companies wanted me in their commercials, and there was a line of breeding knots with my face and name on the packaging. People invited me to parties and paid me to attend, and more movie offers kept streaming in. I'd earned so much in just one year that I could quit porn forever.

Except I didn't want to. I liked it.

Aside from Brian, I worked with another omega director. No more shady deals and shabby motels for film sets. I did high-quality stuff. I even got a say in who I worked with. Rumors were circulating about whether I'd do another heat project and what it would be, and Brian already had a plan. More documentary-like, he said. Just one alpha. This time, he wanted to capture a "sincere connection." He was all about the lurve. I had my doubts, but he was the director.

"Porn doesn't have to be crude, Kirby. It doesn't have to be cynical, right? People want to feel loved. There's so much beauty and depth to physical connection, so why do we always try to downplay that?"

"Because vanilla looks boring on film?"

"I haven't said anything about us doing it vanilla." With that, he winked at me.

Emerson and Burke were having a baby, and Brian and my old co-star Eric were now married. Brian claimed he didn't ask him to, but Eric quit porn. He worked as a PT at a hotel and spa at the harbor.

I dated Dex for a while, but we were a better match on set than off of it. Despite the fact he'd fucked dozens of boys on camera since we got together, he got jealous when I filmed with someone else. In the end, he annoyed me, so I broke it off. I didn't date anyone after that—I was too busy to deal with the mess of relationships.

The biggest change for me was that I didn't wake up in cold sweat anymore after dreaming I was back on the street. And I was pretty damned happy about that.

Then there was Hugh.

We were friends. Sort of. I wished him the best, yet I dreaded the day a clean-cut little omega with a pristine past would show up and snatch him up from under my nose. It was selfish of me, but the rare pining glances he'd given me since Emerson and Burke's wedding were the only even remotely romantic thing in my life. I coveted them like small treasures.

When I got lonely and emotional, I fantasized about how I might quit this business one day. I'd come to the pub, casually ask him out, and he'd smirk at me and call me "kitten" again. Years from now. Maybe.

CHAPTER 1

HUGH

Burke and Emerson had a meeting with their lawyer today, something to do with the shared ownership of the building and pub, so I offered to take Bo for a walk before my shift at the bar. The two-month-old baby was as easy-going as they came, so it was no hassle. If he was fed and the stroller kept moving, he was asleep. Not like Monty, who'd spent the first six months of his life constantly screaming—I still had nightmares about that.

Burke handed me the diaper bag, and I stuffed it into the basket under the carrier.

"I've just changed him, so he should be fine for the next hour, but you never know. He's eaten a lot, so..." Burke grimaced. "Anyway, there's an extra blanket in the basket, and the rain cover is the small bag here." He pointed at the handle. "I checked the weather, and it shouldn't rain, but—"

"Burke." Emerson tugged on Burke's arm. "Let's go."

Burke frowned, peeking at the baby, who was awake

but calm. "He usually falls asleep as soon as you get moving, but if he doesn't—"

"Burke. We need to go." Emerson smiled at me apologetically.

My big alpha boss gave his tiny son one more anxious look. "Just call, okay? I'll leave my phone on."

"I got it, boss, no worries."

"Come on, Burke. Hugh knows what he's doing, and we'll be late."

Burke sighed and let Emerson drag him away. Emerson waved, and they were off, crossing the street.

I figured I'd go the few blocks to the nearby park and maybe buy myself an ice cream there. The leaves were quickly changing colors, winter just around the corner, but it was still unseasonably warm in the afternoons. Walking leisurely, I jiggled the stroller, and Bo nodded off. His eyelids turned that light-lavender hue babies had when they were deeply asleep.

"What the hell are you doing?" I raised my gaze to meet Kirby's mock outraged expression. "Don't tell me there's a baby in it."

As usual, Kirby seemed to own the street. His hair in a stylish mess, long legs in high black boots and skinny jeans, with an open black coat flowing around his lean form, he looked like he'd stepped off a really edgy runway. His shimmery shirt was open a few buttons, revealing his collarbones and an assortment of chains and pearls. He was sexy and glamorous, and like always, the sight of him sent a frisson of desire through my gut.

"Hi, Kirby. How are you today?"

"Fine. I was on my way to the pub to grab a late lunch. Are you closed?"

"No, Derek and Ilja are already there, but it's almost empty this early."

"And what the fuck are you doing with that?" He pointed at the stroller.

"Babysitting for an hour while Burke and Emerson are in a meeting. I was going to grab an ice cream. Wanna join me for a decadent appetizer? I'll bring you back to the pub safe and sound, I promise."

Kirby squinted at the baby, wrinkling his nose. "If I hear a sound from in there, I'm off."

I chuckled. "Okay. You're not one of those people who get excited about babies, are you?"

"What tipped you off? My keep-it-away-from-me face?"

"It was rather obvious, yeah. Are you simply indifferent or downright hostile?"

"Indifferent, I guess," he responded in a serious tone. "They're like any other people, except the jury is still out if they turn out to be crooks or not. I'm not particularly fond of them, but I tolerate this one because he's Emerson's." Kirby peeked into the stroller and a corner of his mouth lifted before he quickly masked it with a frown.

Slowly, we walked up the street, people moving away to make space for us. I figured we might have looked outlandish. A beefy, tattooed guy like me pushing a stroller, with a rock-star-like Kirby by my side. Neither of us looked like somebody's doting parent.

"Do you want kids one day?" I asked, knowing what his answer would be.

"Nope. There are very few things in my life I'm this sure of. You?"

"I feel like I've already done my part."

"I keep forgetting. You're like a dad to Monty." Kirby's tone softened.

"Uncle, but a bit more hands-on than what's standard, I guess. I was there from the day he was born. So he is a bit like my kid."

"And you don't want one of those of your own?"

"Nah. Monty is enough. I love him to bits, but I don't mind being the second in command if you know what I mean."

"I think I do."

We crossed an intersection, and I stopped at a familiar corner.

"Look at that. They boarded it up again," I said, more to myself.

"What?" Kirby paused next to me.

"This place." An old, swirly sign peeked out from under the torn cardboard covering the windows. The door was bolted, and a rusty metal plate reading FOR RENT adorned the frame. "It used to be a famous cocktail bar, been here for decades, but when the owner died a few years back, some distant relatives took over. They changed it into a restaurant, but they weren't very good and closed in a few months. Then it was a coffee shop, but that's gone now too."

"Huh."

I sighed, shaking my head. It was useless to think about it. I gave one last longing look at the fading paint and pushed the stroller away.

"What's the moping look for?" Kirby asked.

"Just foolish dreams of a broke man."

"Tell me."

"I had this idea to rent the place and restore it to its former glory, but that would require a huge investment. I talked about it with Burke, that we could branch out, but with the new baby and the economy today, it's too far-fetched. The pub is doing fine, but he can't risk a big loan, and I totally get it. If it failed, he could lose the entire business."

Kirby was quiet, my speech probably boring him to death.

"Anyway, ice cream."

"Ice cream," he echoed.

We entered the park, leaves crunching under our feet. The ice cream stand was still open like I had hoped. Kirby wanted punch and strawberry mascarpone, and I got plain vanilla.

We sat down on a bench in the sun so we could eat them in peace. I kept jiggling the stroller, and Bo napped like a champ.

"And you can't get a loan either, I guess?"

I blinked. I'd thought Kirby hadn't been listening. "No. Jay and I owe money for my dad's old medical bills. We manage, but it's from paycheck to paycheck. I don't qualify for a business loan, and I can't push Burke to take a risk that could break him."

"Have you talked to Richard?"

"Richard Porter? Burke's friend from college?"

"Yeah. He's like a finance shark. I have no idea what exactly he does, but maybe he could help. From what I know, he's filthy rich."

"Hasn't he moved away?"

"He lives in Ellis Beach, bought a house there and moved in with a boyfriend, a cute kid called Carter. But he still visits."

"I know. I've served him and his boyfriend at the pub.

But we've never really talked beyond orders and a few jokes."

"Couldn't hurt to ask."

"Nah." I wouldn't ask strangers for money. That was just weird.

Kirby licked his ice cream, squinting into the autumn sun. I tried not to stare at his lips, but it was difficult. He pulled a pair of sunglasses out of his pocket and put them on.

"And you and Jay are okay?" he asked after a while, his expression inscrutable.

"Yeah. As I said, it's a bit wobbly from time to time, but we manage."

"I can help, you know." His voice was quiet and oddly insecure. "I don't have enough to buy a cocktail bar with you, but I've been saving up. So if you hit a bump in the road, let me know, okay?"

"That's really generous of you, Kirby. Thanks."

"Well, I mean it. I've never had money before. It's weird. Most of the time, it freaks me out, but my agent hooked me up with an adviser, so I'm getting the hang of it. It would make me feel good if I could help, okay?"

"Okay."

He turned to me, his mouth tense around the corners. I could sense it was important to him that I didn't take his words as an empty promise. "So you will let me know?"

"I will, Kirby."

He smiled, and even though the sunglasses covered his eyes, I could tell it was a true, happy smile. Kirby was gaining control over his life, and it was beautiful to see.

We wouldn't need his help. Jay and I had it all worked out between the two of us. Our budget was tight but bulletproof, with sufficient insurance through Jay's job and meager savings for Monty's education.

But I got why Kirby said what he said, and I wouldn't shit on his offer.

The baby made a faint sound, just a sigh, nothing to worry about, but Kirby shot to his feet.

"We better keep moving, man," he said, eyeing the stroller like it was a bomb about to go off.

Grinning, I scrambled up. "Chill, he's fast asleep." But I grabbed the handle, and we took off toward the busy streets. It was time to go back anyway.

"What's today's special?" Kirby asked when we were nearing the pub.

"Ilja's making goulash."

"Yum."

"You've just had ice cream."

Kirby spread out his arms, his smile wide. "I know! What a wonderful world."

Kirby's metabolism was a mystery. I'd seen him stuff himself with combos and amounts of food that would make me sick for a week, but he washed it down with a beer and asked for seconds.

"I love Ilja's cooking," he enthused. "He's a genius."

"I second that."

Bo woke up just as we were rounding the last corner. He didn't cry, but I sped up anyway. No need to risk it.

Burke was hovering by the door, and as soon as we entered the pub, he snatched the baby from the stroller and cuddled him to his massive chest.

"Hello, little man, was it nice in the park? Yeah? Did you have a good nap?"

Kirby folded his sunglasses, hugged Emerson hello, and headed straight for the bar.

"Thank you so much," Emerson said to me.

"Did it go okay with the lawyer?"

"Yeah. Everything's fine." He looked up at his husband, who was nuzzling the squirming baby. "I'd better feed him, I guess."

Burke handed the baby over, gazing at Emerson longingly when the little omega walked away, presumably to chestfeed in private.

"Thanks, man," Burke said. "And sorry for the, uh, overprotective behavior." He sounded like he was quoting someone, probably his husband. "It was the first time someone babysat for us, and I guess I was more nervous than necessary."

"I'm honored you trusted me." I patted his shoulder. "And it's great to see you happy, boss."

Burke gave me a small, crooked smile. His eyes were shining.

After a quick visit to the back room, I took over from Derek at the bar counter so he could take a break. With a half-empty beer glass in front of him, Kirby scrolled on his phone.

"You've ordered food?"

"Yes." He frowned at the screen. "Ugh. One more beer, and I've got to go. My agent wants me to call him."

I waggled my eyebrows. "A new project?"

Kirby sighed and took a deep swig from his beer. "I'm not allowed to talk about most of it, but obviously, I'll go into heat again just before Christmas. Fah-la-la-la."

"Ah." The unpleasant twinge in my chest had nothing to do with jealousy. Nope.

"Do you already have a co-star for that? Or co-stars?"

"Just one this time. The auditions are about to start."

"So you've got alphas competing for the opportunity to spend the heat with you?"

He wrinkled his nose like he didn't quite like the prospect. "Something like that."

"That sounds…weird."

"I have the final say. Luckily."

"I imagine you'll have plenty to choose from."

Kirby downed his drink without a reply. The topic seemed to spoil his mood, so I didn't push further.

An errant thought passed through my mind as I poured him another beer. The auditions… Were there some entry requirements? Like, what did one have to do to land an audition for a porn flick?

I almost laughed out loud at the bizarre idea.

CHAPTER 2

KIRBY

Tonight, Brian visited me in my newly decorated penthouse—I'd moved again two months ago and now had a view over the harbor—and got straight to business.

"I've heard from Ottavio."

"Ottavio Milani?" The alpha was notorious in the kink community, but I didn't do kink. Not even with a legend like Ottavio. I'd seen snippets of the stuff he'd done. An image of a sobbing omega in the middle of a heat wave popped up in my mind. The omega had been tied to a bench, wearing nipple clamps, his twitching, *empty* ass on display. Ottavio had walked around him, swinging a lubed-up baseball bat. I hadn't watched it to the end. Some omegas enjoyed being tied up during heat and fucked with all kinds of weird items, no shame in that. But I got hives imagining someone treating me like that, in heat no less. I didn't even trust anyone enough to let them tie me up, let alone fuck me with a baseball bat. *No way in hell.*

"His agent has been quite persistent. Ottavio is very

42

keen on working with you and willing to adjust to our concept."

"I'm not doing a heat with Ottavio. Forget it."

Brian gave me a small, knowing smile. "I told them no. Several times." He put his laptop bag onto my coffee table and unzipped it. "Besides, he's already a has-been. He wants to use your fame to boost his dying career, phrasing it as if it's him doing us a favor. So, no. I think we should go with someone new. Someone who won't aspire to over-shadow you but do his absolute best."

He opened the laptop and hit play on the first video. A gorgeous alpha, about thirty, sat on a bed in his underwear. I didn't know him so he must have been either new in town or new to the industry. A muffled question came from somewhere, and he laughed.

"Of course I've seen Kirby Matthews fuck. That's why I'm here, right?"

Brian fast-forwarded the interview, though. Next, he hit play on a clip of the same guy plowing a short, muscular omega from behind. He had a great dick, long with a big fat head. He pulled it out, and the camera zoomed in on the abundance of slick covering it before he jammed it back into the omega's hole at the ideal angle. He knew what he was doing, and sure enough, the rolling thrusts set his partner off big time. The hole began spasming, and the sounds of the omega orgas-ming crackled in the speakers. The video quality was so-so, the lighting shitty, but the fucking? Very nice. Then it cut to the alpha's face...and I grimaced. His eyes said, "I'm a sex god. Look at my amazing dick." I didn't want to spend ten days pretending intimacy with a self-centered prick.

I didn't even have to say anything. "Yes, I know," Brian

said and sighed. "It's a pity because esthetically and athletically, he would be perfect."

The next guy was a little less attractive but a damned machine. I'd never seen anyone move so fast, and I'd thought I'd seen it all. His hips were a blur, and the poor omega's wails made my skin crawl.

"No. Fuck no."

"Are you sure?"

"How about you ram a dildo onto a jackhammer and fuck me with that?"

Brian snickered. "Could be interesting."

"Aren't we looking for a 'genuine connection,' boss?" I said, using my fingers for the quotation marks.

"Yes, we are. That's why I think you might like this one."

He closed the folder and opened another one.

"He's an amateur, so he'd need quite a lot of coaching. A little older than would be ideal, but he doesn't look his age, so who cares. He's never done anything besides a few home clips with fuck buddies. I attached one to this tape so you can see him in action. They wouldn't even let him audition, but I bumped into him on the stairs. He's sweet and funny. Also, had I been single... See for yourself."

"I'm watching."

Brian double-clicked on the clip, and I froze.

Fuck.

Familiar checkered shirt, unforgettable playful eyes, full sexy lips. The shy smile on the worldly face looked unusual. I'd never seen him smile like that before.

"Why are you here?" a voice asked.

"Um. Because I want to be in the movie?"

"Why do you want to be in the movie?"

He blushed. "I...have a thing for filming myself. I've been posting things online, anonymously. But I don't really have to hide it, you know? It's not going to affect my job, so I can just do it. Why not? And of course, I have a thing for Kirby Matthews."

"Why do you think I should give the main role in my most anticipated project to an amateur?" The voice sounded clearer now. It was Brian asking the questions.

The man smiled, mischief in his eyes. I knew that sly sparkle very well. "Because you want someone real."

And cut. Next clip.

Fucking hell.

He lay on his back, his face outside the frame, and a plump omega rode his dick. The image quality was poor, filmed with a phone, but holy hell, it was hot. The omega bounced on that thick shaft, firm, strong hands digging into his hips. The sounds the omega made and the words he uttered said everything. Then Hugh grabbed him and bucked up into him with admirable power, and the omega's moans crested. After a few seconds, he climbed off, and the slick-and-cum-covered cock stood proudly in the center of the image. I'd wanted to see that dick for a long time, and here it was. Fat and veiny. *So fat.* A fucking work of art.

I couldn't keep staring at it if I didn't want to leave a puddle of slick where I was sitting.

"Go back," I told Brian.

He scrolled to the beginning, the video on pause.

"What do you think?" Brian gestured to the screen where Hugh sprawled on the sofa, his shirt open, sleeves rolled up, his tattoos on display, and the bulge in his jeans prominent. Hugh Urban, auditioning for a role in my film. And Brian liked him. Fucking fuck. "You're quiet, Kirby. I'm very much intrigued with this man and would like to hear your opinion."

I rubbed my hands down my face. I wasn't wired to deal with this much temptation, dammit!

"I know him," I let out between my fingers.

"You do? But he's never done a film before."

"Not like that. I know him personally."

"What?" Brian's voice jumped up in pitch and volume.

"He's...like a friend. He's a bartender at a pub that belongs to my best friend's husband."

"Oh."

"Yeah."

"I'm sorry, Kirby. I had no idea. We'll strike him out, of course. I'll let him know immediately. He mentioned that he knew you, but I thought he meant he'd watched your films. Never in a million years would I have let him audition if I had known it was a prank."

"It's not a prank."

Brian froze with his hand on the phone. "Come again."

"He wants to do it. He's not pranking me."

"And...you?"

Ugh.

Okay, so I'd had the hots for the guy for like three years now. But obviously, I didn't date people outside of the industry. It got messy. Hugh was a friend, close to Burke and Emerson, a part of my makeshift family.

"You're hesitating," Brian said. "Why?"

"Nothing has ever happened between us, but we've been flirting for years. I might have been attracted to him... at times." Now that was a lie. I wasn't just attracted to him. Hugh was like a walking talking magnet to me, like catnip to my libido. His voice alone had the power to burrow inside me, squeeze my gut, and make my hole gape open. I had to control my alcohol intake around him, or I wouldn't be able to resist climbing him like a tree.

"So if I did porn too, would you have sex with me?"

"Sure, Hugh. If you were a porn star, I'd fuck your brains out."

Hugh smiled into the camera, frozen in time, and Brian was quiet. I could feel his gaze on me.

"And you are considering—" he began.

"No." I shook my head vehemently. "No. It's a bad idea." *Lord, that dick! You could finally have that... No!*

"Why?"

"I can't. It's too close to home." *Keep convincing yourself.*

Another long pause, and then, "Kirby, I think this might be what we're looking for."

I flashed him a look. Of course Brian would love this, wouldn't he? Letting my private life go up in flames for his 'art.'

"No, Brian." But my voice was weak. Why was my voice weak?

The excitement in Brian's eyes grew with each passing second, and I knew I was screwed.

"This is perfect. You have a crush on each other. Can you imagine how it'll look on camera? He's as unpretentious as they come, Kirby. This could turn out amazing. He'll need a lot of coaching, but that's what we have Walter for. Cameron will do a few sessions with him so he gets used to the angles and lights. I'm tempted to do a test run. Like a trial before the heat."

Warmth pooled in my belly. No, I wouldn't be able to resist. I was *so fucking screwed.*

"You want him to fuck me on camera before the heat to see if he can pull it off?"

"Exactly."

At first, the idea horrified me. But on a second thought, and on a third... The image of Hugh's erect cock covered with cum flashed through my mind. The memory of his scent when we'd danced at Burke's Pub joined the image.

"So?" Brian prompted.

"I'll think about it."

"Let me know tomorrow."

"Okay."

As soon as the door clicked shut behind Brian, I called the doorman to order me a cab. Then I dashed into the shower. I acted on autopilot; a quick scrub-down, my favorite coconut shampoo, my jasmine-scented fluffy towel, a neutral deodorant, and a dab of cream under my eyes. Lip gloss. Salt-water spray. A quick blow-dry.

During my short life, I'd been dirty without access to a decent bathroom for years on end. Now I showered two or three times a day. I was addicted to the feeling of freshly washed cotton on my chest. I loved how stiff clean socks were when I pulled them on. The sensation of silk underwear sliding up my moisturized, hairless legs... I'd become a prince, and so what? A quick swipe over my shoes with the sponge, my pin-striped jacket, keys, phone.

Heart pounding, I jumped up and down in the elevator.

"Your taxi is outside, Mr. Matthews," the doorman said as I passed him in a hurry.

"Thanks, Brandon. Have a good night."

"You too, Mr. Matthews."

Fifteen minutes later, I pushed open the door to Burke's Pub, and there he was. Standing behind the bar in one of his too-small T-shirts, his massive arms and tattoos on display, his shaved head nodding to the beat, he looked like a wet dream. Or a mean bouncer.

Hugh's eyes widened when he saw me. My face must have made it clear that I knew what he'd been up to. He finished pouring a beer and handed it over to a customer.

"Derek, I'll be right back," he said to the other bartender, who looked a little confused but nodded.

Then Hugh rounded the counter and gestured for me to follow him. We went through a narrow hallway, passing the stairs that led up to Burke and Emerson's place, and ended up in a tiny office.

Hugh folded his arms over his chest and sat on the edge of the messy table.

"So I guess you've heard, huh?"

"About your audition? Yes. Brian told me."

"How mad are you?"

I should be mad. I should be unhinged with fury. Or should I?

"I don't fucking know."

I rubbed a hand down my face. What was my problem? Oh yeah.

"It's porn, Hugh. Do you have any idea what you're getting yourself into?"

"A bit, yeah."

"Once it's out there, you can't take it back."

"It's not like I'll ever aspire to become a lawyer or a doctor, Kirby. And my current boss sure won't care."

"No, Burke won't. But many people in your life will judge you for it."

"Not the important ones."

I groaned. "Why, Hugh?"

"It's up to you, Kirby. You can say no. I didn't tell you I was trying to get in, which was shady of me, but I knew you'd be against it before I even tried. Ultimately though, you have the last word. You can say no, and I'll never mention it again. It won't change anything between us, I swear."

I can say no. I can. Say no. Just say no.

"Why?"

Hugh squeezed his eyes shut and blew out a heavy breath.

"Why, Hugh? You owe me honesty."

"Complete honesty?"

"Is there any other kind?"

Bracing his hands on the edge of the table, he lifted his eyes to mine. "Several reasons. I do like filming myself while having sex, and I've uploaded a few clips online, which Brian might have told you. So it's not my first rodeo, just the first time I'd be showing my face. So, yeah. I think I would get off on it. Which is...the least important reason."

"Go on."

"Money. That's a big one."

Hugh lived with his little brother who had a kid. And I knew they struggled financially. I couldn't shit on that. I'd be the worst hypocrite in the world if I berated him for wanting to have sex for money.

"And then there's you." He smiled the familiar self-deprecating smile, his eyes gentle, and I had to look away.

"Dammit, Hugh."

"I've always wanted you."

"This is possibly the most screwed-up way to get into my pants anyone has ever attempted."

"Remember the guy who tattooed your face on his chest and bought you a plane ticket to Brazil?"

"Okay, you're the second most insane one."

My palms were damp, and I could hear my own heartbeat. A part of me already knew I'd do it. Which was infuriating.

"Are you mad?" he asked.

At myself, yes. "Hugh, I know you. You're not the type for this. You might think you are, but you'll hate it. There's nothing even remotely romantic or affectionate about fucking on camera. It's barely even proper sex. It's acting. Work. They take what you think is an act of love and chop it up like a lamb on the butcher's table. It's not real. It's all pretend. Don't you get it?"

"Isn't that why Brian chose me? Because he wants it to look real?"

I shot him a glare, and he lifted his palms apologetically. "Just because Brian wants it to look a certain way," I said, "doesn't make the whole thing any less fake."

The flash of hurt on Hugh's face cut into my heart, but I wouldn't let it show. I wouldn't be able to tell him no, so I needed him to back out of it himself.

Except Hugh Urban had already decided, just like I had. He pushed off the table and took a few steps toward me. I was fucking trembling on the inside. No man had ever affected me as much as Hugh, and now he wanted me during my heat. I was screwed. Doomed. The end.

His heavy, warm palm rested on the side of my neck while he held my gaze.

"What do you want, Kirby? Because that's what it all comes down to. It's *your heat*. Do you want to do it with me?"

It would be the first time I'd be spending my heat with someone I even remotely cared about. My heart ached with the idea. *There'll be cameras, boy, so don't get too excited.*

"Do you want me, Kirby?"

Those eyes.

51

Pleading, kind, yearning... He moved his hand higher up, his thumb lifting my jaw a little. I wanted to kiss him so badly I could weep.

His gaze flicked to my lips, and I bit the bottom one to stop myself from diving into his mouth. I put my palm on his chest, but instead of pushing him away, I only caressed him through the threadbare T-shirt. Hugh was built like a bull. Hard muscle, a healthy layer of fat, broad chest, bulging pectorals, his stomach rounded but firm... And now I knew how thick his cock was.

Of course I wanted him. I'd always wanted him. The more I knew him, the more I was convinced *he* shouldn't want *me*.

"I'm not good for you, Hugh," I whispered.

He raised one eyebrow, his lips curving into a crooked smile. "Let me be the judge of that." He leaned closer, and his breath fanned my face.

Loud stomps coming from the hallway made me jump back. A second later, Burke filled the doorway.

"Oh. Hi, Kirby." He looked at Hugh, then at me, and at Hugh again. He slapped the doorframe, looking puzzled. "I'm interrupting." Taking a step back, he was about to leave again.

It was now or never.

"No, it's okay. I have to go. Bye."

I ducked under Burke's arm and ran.

CHAPTER 3

HUGH

Brian called me the next day, all excited, wanting me to come to the studio and sign the contract. Kirby must have said yes. I messaged Kirby if he wanted to meet up and talk some more, but he replied he was busy.

He'd avoided me ever since, and I would have demanded an explanation, but in a way, I got it. We knew we would end up having sex with each other. We knew when and how. I suspected that if I saw him in private before that, I wouldn't be able to keep my hands off him, and maybe Kirby knew and was trying to keep things friendly and professional.

During the time we waited for Kirby's heat, Brian scheduled a couple of sessions with a heat consultant— one by myself and one together with Kirby. I didn't think it was needed, but since I got reimbursed for the hours, I gladly took it. Getting paid for chatting about sex with an expert sounded like a neat deal.

I'd heard the name before, so I knew the guy was a big

shot. On the subway to meet him at the studio, I scrolled through an article about him. He used to be a heat teacher. *The* heat teacher, apparently. He'd worked for—meaning he'd fucked and knotted—celebrities, sons of high-flying businessmen, and even foreign aristocracy. Allegedly, he'd guided His Excellency Caleb Massoud Bernal through his first heat, and they'd remained friends to this day. There were rumors that Walter Sébastien met his current husband on the job, which would have been all kinds of shady. But since he'd quit hands-on heat support as soon as they'd gotten together, was now happily married to the guy, and they were raising a kid together, who cared?

Sébastien was an alpha in his forties, his looks unremarkable, but once he opened his mouth, you knew he had brains. He immediately asked me to call him Walter and shook my hand with a warm, firm grip.

"Do you know why you're here?" He lounged on a low, bright-red sofa, his understated casual attire all in shades of black and dark gray. He held his cup of coffee with both hands.

"Because Brian is a control freak?"

He chuckled. "That, too. Have you thought about what's expected of you on the set?"

That was fairly straightforward. "Take care of Kirby and make it look hot. Cameron has already been nagging me about positions, lights, and camera angles."

"The make-it-look-hot part is Brian's domain. I don't give a damn about that. But you'll be taking care of Kirby, and my job is to ensure you do it well. You're what, forty? Have you helped someone through a heat before?"

"Thirty-nine, and yes. Four times."

"Same partner or several?"

"Same."

"Are you still together?"

I blew out a breath. I didn't want to talk about it, but it seemed I'd have to. "I wouldn't be here, would I?"

Walter tilted his head to the side as if appraising me from another angle. "Sex workers do have private lives just like everybody else. They have relationships and families. Since you're about to enter the business right at the top level, you should update your knowledge and inspect your prejudice before you say something thoughtless to someone who'd care. Like Kirby."

"I hear you. I didn't mean to offend anyone. It's been Kirby himself telling me he didn't have relationships with anyone outside the industry."

Narrowing his eyes at me, Walter took a long gulp of his coffee. "Those four heats. How did that go?"

I should have known he wouldn't let it slide. "Good. My ex had mild heats and short recoveries. We used protection and avoided breeding."

"Did you enjoy it?"

"Sure."

"Where's your ex now?"

"Lives down in San Diego with another omega."

Walter blinked. "I'm sorry."

"It's okay. It took him a while, but when he figured out he didn't really like alphas all that much, we parted ways amicably."

"Did you love him?"

"Aren't we supposed to talk about heats?"

"Your experiences have shaped your current attitude. I'm just doing basic reconnaissance."

I blew out a breath. "I did love him. It hurt, but it was a long time ago, and I've reconciled myself to it. It wasn't anybody's fault, just bad luck. I haven't had a serious relationship since, but I'm not opposed to it."

"What is your relationship to Kirby?"

"He's a regular at the pub I work at, and we're friends."

"How did he react when he found out you were auditioning for the role?"

"He was surprised, but when I explained, he agreed to it."

"How did you explain?"

"Told him the truth."

"Which was?"

"That I really need the money, have a mile-wide exhibitionist streak, and that I've always been attracted to him."

Smiling as if my response satisfied him, he put the empty cup onto a side table next to the sofa.

"I was present for some parts of the filming when Kirby's first heat movie was made. I also had a few conversations with Kirby. His heats are intense, and he needs breeding and fisting to go through them. I've sent you some materials via email that I expect you to read through —just general information about intense heats and the techniques you can use when things get rough in the middle. Thing is"—he paused, squinting at me—"Brian is after authenticity. Visible enjoyment, yes, but also a connection. You being friends and attracted to each other is a good start. Kirby is instructed not to fake anything for the camera, and you must learn to play his body. Read his reactions and adjust."

My brain was still stuck on the fisting, and I had to recap what he'd said.

"Are you following?"

"Yeah. It's like with any lover. Figure out what makes him feel good and keep doing it, right?"

Walter laughed. "It's ten days of intense heat sex, Hugh, with the omega of everyone's dreams that you've had a crush on for years, I suspect. It'll be nothing like with any lover you've had before, and we both know it."

I swallowed.

"Are you in love with him?"

"No." I said it too loud and too fast.

He smiled kindly, with only a little bit of condescension in his gaze.

"Imagine it's the sixth day, you're locked in breeding with him after watching him come a hundred times already, his pheromones have melted your brain to mush, and the thought of him ever leaving you for just a minute makes you want to vomit or smash things. Anytime you close your eyes, you dream about sucking his chest milk and kissing his pregnant belly and how you want to massage his feet. He sighs, and you're about to cry from how beautiful that little sound is." He paused. "Now imagine a camera zooming in on your face while you feel like that."

I had nothing. The fear and discomfort made me mute.

"Did you feel that type of connection with your ex?"

Looking down at my hands, I shook my head. "As I said, his heats were mild, and I've never bred him. Why are you telling me this?" Did Kirby ask him to scare me off?

"Because you need to take it seriously. Feelings may arise that will make your role difficult. However professional you both aspire to be, you won't be able to uphold it during one-on-one heat sex. Heat with someone who gets as immersed in it as Kirby does can be a life-altering experience."

"Even on a porn set."

"Yes. Even on a porn set."

"Why are *you* doing this?"

He shrugged. "Money?"

"Bullshit. Like me, you're not here just for the dollars."

"You're right. I'm not. Pornography can be toxic and destructive—both the process and the end result. There's no point in censoring it because people will always find their way around any rules you might put up. But by giving out quality erotic content, you can empower and liberate people. I support Brian because I admire the work he's done."

"Um, can I have another question?"

"It's what I'm here for."

"Let's say a performer develops feelings for a partner on set. Do you have any advice about how to handle it? How to prepare for it?"

He was quiet for a long moment, scrutinizing me with unpleasant focus. "It depends. But to you, I'd say, don't panic and let it flow."

"Let it flow?" That was quite lousy advice from a renowned expert.

"You won't be able to do anything about your feelings for Kirby during the heat itself. Just let it flow. Channel it into the intimacy between you two. During his heat, Kirby will only appreciate it. Once the heat is over, you'll have time to truly inspect your emotions and deal with the consequences."

Consequences. Like a broken heart and a ruined friendship. "Am I stupid for doing this?"

Chuckling, Walter leaned back against the sofa cushions. "Yes. But you're going to do it anyway, even if I advise you to back out. In your place, I'd do the same."

"And this is what Brian's paying you for?"

"I'm worth every penny," he announced and winked.

I couldn't help but laugh with him.

"The next session will be with Kirby. Do you have something you'd like to bring up while it's just you and me?"

"There's one thing I wanted to ask. I have...um... About my ex." Why did this have to be so hard to talk about?

"Yes?"

"He experienced severe discomfort the first couple of times I knotted him. For a moment, it even got painful for him. After that, we only did it in missionary position because that was the only way he could relax into it."

Walter blinked rapidly and scratched his ear. "Your partner complained about the size of your knot?"

"My penis is...above average in girth."

The corners of Walter's mouth twitched. "I'm sure Kirby won't mind."

I squinted at him. "Because he's a porn star?"

"You said your ex's heats were mild and that he was more attracted to omegas than alphas, is that right?"

"Yes."

"Well, Kirby's heats are intense. I'm sure he'll only appreciate the extra girth." And he winked.

Lord, I needed out of here. Not that he was in any way annoying, but the sex talk was making me all kinds of uncomfortable in all the wrong places, especially considering I was alone in a room with another alpha. "Okay. That's it, then."

"Lovely." Did Walter's eyes flicker to my groin? "In case something occurs to you, we have another session booked with Kirby. We'll have time to cover any topics we might have missed today."

"Okay." I stood and rolled my shoulders. I ached to go

running or swimming, but instead, I had eight hours of tending bar in front of me.

"It's been a pleasure," Walter said. "If it helps, I think Brian made an excellent choice with you."

"Thanks, I guess?"

Walter chuckled. "See you next week, Hugh."

"See you."

MONTY WAS ASLEEP, and Jay and I sat at the kitchen table. My little brother's worried eyes searched my face. He looked so tired, with dark circles under his eyes and pale cheeks. I felt guilty for keeping him up late, but we needed to talk.

"How much will it be?" he asked cautiously.

I pitched my voice low, even though I wanted to shout it. "Thirty-seven thousand after tax."

Jay pushed off the table and groaned. "Fuck, Hugh. Is that even legal?"

"It's not usual porn," I explained. "It's heat porn, ten days of filming, and with Kirby Matthews. And yes, everything is done properly with insurance, health exams, and an NDA. I'm only allowed to tell you because we share a household and economy. You can't tell anyone else. If the film does well, I'll get a bonus after six months. Could be anything between another ten or fifty."

"Thousand dollars?" Jay looked still horrified, like I was telling him I'd started cooking and selling meth. "This is insane."

"Brian, the director, is a big deal. He's the one who made Kirby an international star. He says that if the film is a success, I'll be known in certain circles and that could open other opportunities."

"Like more movies?" Jay's mouth curled in a disapproving grimace.

"No, you prude. Like events and advertising."

"But only those thirty-seven are sure."

"Yes."

Jay blew out a breath. "It's a lot of money, and it would make a helluva difference for us. But is it really worth it, Hugh? Everybody in your life will know." He pointed a finger at me. "Even Monty."

I winced. Yeah. Monty would find out one day that Uncle Hughie made a porno. On the other hand... "It's with Kirby. Not just anyone. I wouldn't do it with anyone else but him. And besides, do you think less of Kirby because he does porn and used to be homeless?"

"No. Of course not," he said defensively.

I made a 'duh' face, and Jay rolled his eyes.

"Don't you have other ways to get into his pants?" he asked.

"No." I laughed humorlessly. "Believe me, I've tried."

Jay shook his head. "You're nuts."

"For wanting to make porn or for doing it to get to sleep with Kirby?"

"Both."

"But I'll take it. Do you know why?"

"No, but you'll tell me."

"Because I'll get to sleep with Kirby!" I whisper-shouted.

The look my little brother gave me was no doubt intended to be withering, but on his boyish face, it looked adorable. "Seriously?"

"Sounds better than 'I'm fucking for money to pay off a giant debt my dad left behind when he died of cancer.'

Besides, I am excited about being with Kirby during his heat. Not gonna lie."

"Of course you are. But what does Kirby think?"

"He's okay with it."

"Is he?" Jay tilted his head to the side and squinted at me.

"We talked, and then Brian texted me Kirby said yes."

"I still think it's crazy." My little brother leaned back in his chair and rested his head on the wall. He looked truly exhausted.

"Go to bed, Jaybird."

He nodded, closing his eyes. "I just need to stand up first."

Grabbing his hand, I hauled him up. "You're so tiny. How are we even related?"

"Ha-ha."

"See you tomorrow, Jay."

"Goodnight, Hugh." He gave me a hug, and I ruffled his hair like I used to do when he was a kid. He shoved me away.

"Dork."

"Love you too."

CHAPTER 4

KIRBY

After not seeing him in a while, I all but ate Hugh up with my eyes. He wore a simple T-shirt with a discreet *Burke's Pub* stamp on the front. Again, it seemed to be one size too small, and his beefy arms stretched the sleeves to capacity. Those tattoos alone warranted a scenic route—ocean waves, birds, gnarled branches, night sky, a small boy chasing a balloon, a silhouette of an old man on a bench in front of a cottage... Like a kaleidoscope of memories. I could strip him naked, trace all of them, and have him tell me all the stories behind them.

Walter Sébastien entered the room, jerking me back into reality.

Work. This is work.

In today's session, we would share our preferences and limits. Even though I was trying to avoid Hugh before the filming, I had to admit it was probably necessary for us both to be present and talk it through. Besides, Walter would act as a buffer between us.

When we settled down, Walter stretched his arms above his head and glanced from me to Hugh and back. I got a flashback to my sessions with Walter two years back when he nitpicked through my so-called traumatic experiences from my time on the streets. I'd hated those sessions, but they did help. I braced myself for another round of unpleasant truths.

"So. Brian thinks we can do this in one sitting since you already know each other. Hugh, have you read the documents I've sent you?"

"About intense heats and aftercare, yes. But I'll go through them again before the filming."

"Good. Kirby, you've done this already, so we won't waste time on the basic stuff and get right to the fun part."

There was nothing even remotely fun about this. I was exposed and didn't like it. Hugh's invasion of my work life felt a little like I let him watch me going to the toilet. He knew about the nasty bits, but did he have to see it with his own eyes? "I'm curious about what you mean by fun," I said, not even trying to mask the sarcasm.

"You'll see." Walter winked at me, then turned to Hugh. "What can you tell Kirby about your alpha based on how you acted toward your sex partners during heat?"

I had to admit it was interesting to see the big man flustered. His cheeks went bright red, and I bit back a grin. "Um. Like what?"

"For example, do you feel the urge to protect your partner? To dominate him?"

"Doesn't everyone?"

Walter laughed. "Okay. This might take more than one session. Affected by the pheromones of an omega in heat, most alphas experience the need to take control of the mating situation. Some act protective and caring, some tend to get aggressive and possessive. How does your need for dominance present itself?"

Hugh's eyes flicked from Walter to me and back. "Like during heat sex?"

"Yes, Hugh, during heat sex," Walter said with infinite patience. I could see now what he'd meant—this was super fun.

Hugh squirmed in his seat, looking anywhere but at me and Walter. "I like to be on top. Even if an omega rides me, I get an urge to hold him and thrust up."

"Can you come and knot without it?"

"I've always only knotted when I was the one setting the pace, so to speak."

"This is the stuff Kirby needs to know. Good. When you say 'hold him,' is it more like a hug or do you enjoy leaving bruises, physically restraining your partner, choking, or covering his mouth?"

Hugh looked horrified. "Choking? No!"

Walter smiled benevolently. "It's not uncommon. Some omegas like it."

Hugh looked at me, eyes wide. "Do you?"

"I like being manhandled but not tied up or otherwise restrained. Not being able to move during a peaking heat wave can make me panic. You can grab my throat and squeeze shortly but always let me breathe normally. I prefer no pain if I can avoid it."

"Okay." He seemed to be relieved.

"Hugh, I'm going to conclude that you're more of a protective alpha," Walter said. "Correct?"

"Um. I guess? I do like it when an omega seems sort of helpless when I'm, uh, having sex with him. I want him to... like really need me. But I don't enjoy inflicting pain of any kind."

"You're a large man. Would you say that you're aware and in control of your own strength?"

Hugh sat up straight and folded his arms over his chest. "I'd like to think so."

"Based on...?" Walter's eyebrows flew up expectantly.

"I've never had an incident that would indicate something else, in or out of bed. I work at a pub. Sometimes I have to physically remove people. I've never hurt anyone, and I solve conflicts with aggressive drunks on a daily basis."

"He's good at that," I said. I'd seen Hugh in action many times. "Remains calm. It's basically impossible to provoke him into violence."

Walter seemed pleased with that. "How about knotting? Do you like it?"

Hugh sputtered. "Of course."

"You'd be surprised how many alphas find growing a knot uncomfortable. Would you say that it happens unexpectedly, or do you feel it coming?"

"I can somewhat control it, I think." He scratched his neck, staring at his knees. "When I feel the urge, like a tingle at the base, then I can slow down or speed up, depending on circumstances."

"That's excellent. You told me that your knot gets very large and that it caused your ex-partner discomfort in the past. Kirby, do you see a problem with that?"

Ooh-la-la. It seemed I was in for a treat. "How large?"

"I don't know."

I frowned at Hugh. "You don't know?"

He laughed, exasperated. "Not like I've ever measured it. It always happened *inside* another person."

"Well, your dick is thick." The scene from the audition

video was etched into my memory. "So I assume your knot will be in proportion?"

Hugh's blue eyes grew wide. "You've seen my dick?" he rasped and coughed, covering his mouth with his hand.

"It's impressive, congratulations. Brian always shows me the audition videos."

Hugh cleared his throat. "Course he does."

"I don't see a problem with taking a large knot, though."

"No?"

I smiled and patted his knee. "Not a problem at all."

Walter seemed to suppress a smile. "Kirby, if you ask Hugh for a knot, do you want him to do it immediately?"

I grinned. I loved this session—it was the best one yet. "No."

Again, Hugh looked at me with surprise. He was such an easy target. Between Walter and me, we could tease him for hours. "No? Then how—"

"I like to get a little desperate. When I start begging for a knot, I'm still enjoying the buildup. You can drag it out and edge me. You can even verbally deny me. When I turn quiet and whimper more than moan, I need it badly."

Hugh's mouth was slightly open as he stared at me. It was difficult to say with the lighting, but his pupils seemed just a tad dilated.

"And after the knotting? Can I keep fucking you?" he asked quietly.

"Yeah. I don't like it if you pull out too much so the knot starts stretching my rim from the inside, but if you keep the thrusts short and deep, I'm a happy guy."

He blinked. His ears got so red they could signal traffic.

"Can you come again when you're knotted?" Walter asked.

"Yes," we replied in unison, and I chuckled.

"Wonderful. Brian will be overjoyed. Kirby, give Hugh your main erogenous zones."

"My nipples. Big time. It's the only place where I like a bit of a sting. Sucking, pinching, biting... Anything goes, especially during heat. I like having my ass muscles kneaded and massaged. Light spanking is okay but only on my ass, hate it on my inner thighs or taint. Bellybutton. Earlobes. The back of my neck. I'm extremely ticklish, but once I'm sufficiently aroused, light touches on my sides or here drive me wild." I tapped the crook of my neck and could practically feel Hugh's gaze there like a laser beam.

"Perfect. Hugh?"

"Um." He paused, swallowing audibly. "My balls?" he croaked.

I burst out laughing, and Hugh looked at me accusingly. "What?"

"Nothing. You're precious, dude."

"Fuck off." The corner of his mouth twitched with a suppressed smile.

Walter was smirking too. "Something else besides your testicles?"

"I...don't know. I'm usually the one doing all the touching."

"Something to explore, then. Have you ever fisted a partner during heat?"

Hugh shook his head as if he was sleepy and trying to wake up. Then he dragged his hands down his face. "Can we take a break?"

"Do you need to pee?" I asked innocently.

"No. But a glass of cold water would be nice."

His expression blank, Walter just gestured to the windowsill where a full carafe and glasses stood.

"Oh. Thanks."

"Sorry to be such a tyrant," Walter said, "but I have a client right after this, so I need to be efficient. Are you okay if we continue for twenty more minutes?"

"Sure. Go ahead." Hugh downed his water glass, refilled it, and handed me one before sitting back down next to me. He was a little closer than before, and his body heat radiated all the way to me. "So fisting," he said, deadpan. "Never done that either." He looked at his hand, stretching his fingers, his expression worried. He did have huge hands. I got just a little wetter looking at them. I could picture it vividly, his arm sticking out of my body, skin drenched with slick, my legs shaking, underbelly bulging…

"Kirby might need it during the most intense phase. It allows you to stimulate his erection with your mouth, which has a definite soothing effect for him, not to mention alphas usually enjoy the taste of heat cum. Compared to knotting, a fist can be more powerful. You can angle your knuckles so they rub his gland, pump in and out, and penetrate the mouth to the womb with your fingers. I'll send you a video on how to position your hand so we avoid even minor injuries. Watch it in private since it passes as pornography even though it's instruction. Also, pay attention to your manicure." Hugh inspected his nails. They were short and clean. "Kirby, thoughts or comments on fisting?"

"From the third day onward, I should be open enough for it. I quite like it. Breeding orgasms, especially from fisting, sometimes make me twitch. But if Hugh is up for sucking me off at the same time, I'll melt into the mattress."

Hugh said nothing, but his breathing got louder.

"Let's talk breeding orgasms then, shall we? Kirby, you

have the contraceptive device inserted, so that's covered. Hugh, have you ever bred a partner?"

"No," he replied, sounding exhausted.

I was starting to feel sorry for him.

WHEN THE CONSULTATION ended ten minutes later, Hugh ran out of there like a bat from hell. I couldn't blame him. I was hot and bothered myself. I said a quick goodbye to Walter and headed straight for the gym where I took a long cold shower before spending forty-five minutes on the rowing machine and stairs.

My plan for the night was a slow, loving session with my biggest dildo and then ice cream in front of the TV. A message from Hugh thwarted that.

Hugh: *Can we talk?*

Me: *Now?*

Hugh: *I could come by your place if you send me the address.*

I could have come up with yet another excuse, but I couldn't avoid him forever. Actually, starting next week, I wouldn't be able to avoid him at all. Instead of satisfying my constant yearning to be near him, seeing him today had only unsettled me.

Me: *Okay. Seaview Ave 34A. I'll call our doorman to let you in.*

My stomach felt iffy. Did I put too much mayo on my

salad? It was my weakness. Garlic mayo and cheese. *Any* kind of cheese. I still wasn't used to buying and eating whatever I wanted, and sometimes I went a little overboard.

Ouch, definitely iffy. After a quick run to the toilet, I showered and downed a diet coke. Maybe it was the upcoming heat. I was already more slick than usual as my body cleansed itself on the inside in preparation. It made stuff down there empty and fresh without the hassle of douching, so I wouldn't complain. I put on lace briefs, canary yellow, and told myself it was for the confidence boost and not because of the man coming to visit. *Yeah, right.*

Fussing with my hair in front of the hallway mirror, I had to admit that mayo or heat had nothing to do with my upset stomach. I was nervous. Me, Kirby Matthews, nervous because of an alpha I was about to fuck. Without Walter Sébastien to keep it professional, I was a sitting duck. I hadn't been this twisted up about sex since I was a teen. It was vaguely humiliating.

The intercom beeped, and I dashed to the door.

"Mr. Matthews, your visitor is here."

"Thank you, Brandon. Send him up."

Okay, deep breaths. It was just Hugh, an old friend and a future coworker. No need to freak out. Did I hear the elevator? No. That must have been another floor. But now? The quiet ding was unmistakable.

I opened the door to my apartment, and there he stood.

He looked delicious. I wanted to run my hands all over that shorn head. See, Hugh was the kind of guy who just took things as they came. If he could do something to fix a problem, he simply did it. If he couldn't do shit to change it, he shrugged and moved on. So a year ago, when I was sitting by the bar having a beer, he bent his head and asked if his long hair looked weird at the top because it had been thinning so much. I said yeah, a bit, but only from some angles. Didn't look bad per se, but more skin was showing. When I saw him a few days later, he had a buzz cut all over, and it suited him madly, especially together with the scruffy stubble.

Now, instead of telling him he looked incredibly hot, I raised my eyebrows at him.

"Still running around in T-shirts? It's barely fifty degrees outside."

He shrugged. "I took the subway. Can I come in?"

"Sure."

I stepped back to let him pass and closed the door behind him.

Hugh whistled. "Wow, Kirby. This is...wow." He looked around the living room and walked toward the glass wall overlooking the harbor. A ferry was just leaving toward the islands, and the moon glowed silver, mirrored in the ocean. "This is amazing. How much is the rent on this place?"

"I wouldn't know. I bought it."

"Fuck me." Hugh laughed, shaking his head. "Should I have asked Brian for more money?"

I stuffed my hands into my jean pockets. Money talk embarrassed me. "Most of what I earn nowadays is from events and advertising. The heat sex toys started it, but then I did the underwear ads in the spring. I'm still working with that agency."

"Ah. Makes sense. Well, your home looks awesome. Congratulations."

"Drink?"

"No. I'm good. I just want to talk."

I braced myself. "Then talk."

Hugh turned away from the view and mirrored my position with his hands in his pockets. Except he seemed to take up the entire room while I felt like I was shrinking. "You've been avoiding me. Why?"

Trying to buy myself some time, I sat down on the sectional, but Hugh remained standing.

"I was busy."

"Bullshit." His tone wasn't mean, just matter-of-fact. "You're at the pub at least once a week but never on my shifts."

I winced. I'd been rather transparent.

"Have you changed your mind?" he asked. "Because that's okay. You can always change your mind, Kirby. Just tell me. Don't avoid me."

I looked down at my knees. My jeans had holes in them, much like they used to, but this time, I bought them like this. Designer nonsense. "I haven't changed my mind. You?"

"No."

He still waited for my explanation—I could feel his gaze on me.

"I didn't want it to become awkward." *And I need to stay away because I'm afraid of how much I want you.*

Slowly, Hugh sat down next to me, keeping two feet of distance between us.

"I feel like I should give you an out in case you want to cancel. That's why I'm here. So if you want to back out—"

"I don't want that."

"What's making you worry, Kirby? Aside from the fact that next week, we'll be making heat porn together."

I gave out a broken laugh. "Aside from that...nothing."

"I've been reading up on intense heats and talking to Walter. I'm prepared for all sorts of things. And there'll be staff to take care of anything I might miss. I'm not going to fuck up, Kirby. You say it's work, and you're right, but you're important to me. I want to make it good for you."

I squeezed my eyes shut. Only one whiff of his scent made my head spin. I'd built this up in my head, and now the big day was coming closer... Was I going to freak out big time? On camera? During heat?

"Kirby?"

Peering up at him, I blurted out the truth. "I'm nervous, okay?"

He blinked. "Because it's heat? Walter said that filming porn during heat is—"

"I'm nervous because it's you."

"Me?"

He wasn't getting it, which was probably for the best.

"Can we fuck now? I need to get it over with." Oh jeez, my brain. I wanted to kick myself.

Hugh froze next to me, and I looked at his stunned expression from the corner of my eye. I could feel my pulse hammering in my ears.

"Did I say that out loud?"

"You did."

"Shit."

And then his hands were on me. His broad, hot hands. He gripped my neck, which in itself would have me melting, but his other palm warmed my lower back, fingers dipping under my waistband, and my meager restraint was gone with a quiet poof.

He hauled me close, and I didn't even realize I gasped before his tongue was in my mouth. I moaned in glorious defeat.

The first and last time I'd kissed Hugh, we'd been both inebriated, but I still remembered it as the hottest kiss of my life. He pulled me to him, his chest against mine, he growled into my mouth, and yeah... The first one was now second place. I arched into his grip, rubbing my nipples against him, and he fisted the hair at my nape. Our tongues slid against each other, teeth clanked, and I wanted him to fucking eat me alive.

I liked sex. Since I no longer had to do it in back alleys and parks with any lowlife who'd just gotten his weekly pay, I'd learned to relax into it and enjoy it.

But this was something else. Kissing Hugh, I got distinctly aware of *my womb* and how empty it was. I'd never before felt this yearning, this aching, hollow need deep inside me that made me want to roll over and push my ass up as if I were in heat already.

Keeping a firm grip on my hair, Hugh unbuttoned my jeans with his left hand and gave them a firm tug. Of course, the tight material got stuck around my hips, so I quickly pushed them down and off my feet. Hugh palmed my cock and pulled away from the biting kiss, looking down.

"Oh wow," he rasped, brushing his hands over the glowing yellow fabric.

I quickly tossed my T-shirt, and he slithered down my body, moving way too fast for such a big, bulky man. He nuzzled my groin through my briefs. The lace stretching over my hard dick didn't leave anything to the imagination. Hugh ran his nose along my erection and lifted my thighs to spread my legs open. Then he buried his face between my ass cheeks, inhaling through the thin lace.

"They're wet."

"Uh-huh." I couldn't form words.

"Gorgeous."

He placed kisses all over them, on my ass cheeks, balls,

inner thighs, his lips brushing my skin through the small openings in the lace. My legs shook.

"Hugh, please."

Then he slowly, very slowly, pulled them off. My cock bounced off my underbelly, and I spread my legs wider, showing him everything. I'd never been as needy in my entire life, and I was still at least a week away from my heat.

Eyes pinned on my most vulnerable bits, Hugh sniffed the lace briefs and stuffed them into his back pocket.

With only a tip of a finger, he traced my rim. A shiver ran through me, and I mewled pathetically. The fleeting touch was electric.

"Please," I whimpered.

What was it about this man that made me beg? Alphas all over the country were ready to pay half of their property and give up a kidney to have sex with me. I didn't have to beg anyone for anything.

His expression predatory, eyes almost black, Hugh dipped a fingertip inside me and circled gently.

I cried out, the needy high-pitched sound echoing through the apartment. My hips shot up from the sofa cushion, my body vibrating with want.

"So horny." Hugh dragged his T-shirt over his head, revealing his phenomenal torso, and I felt a dollop of slick escape from my hole. When he began working on his jeans, I had to bite my tongue to keep myself from whining. My insides ached for friction, and I couldn't wait to feel the stretch of this man's cock sliding inside me.

Except Hugh must have decided to torture me. I only got a glimpse of his erection before he shuffled down and hugged my hips. He licked the slick I'd leaked and pressed a firm kiss to my rim. The ache turned into an almost pain.

"Fuck me. Please, Hugh, fuck me."

I was going insane. How was it possible to want someone this much? Was the heat coming early? Was it all the buildup? I'd wanted him for years and now—

"Oh yes!"

Thick, hot tongue. Deep. Right there. Swirling, curling, sliding alongside the front wall of my hole, suckling lips... The slurping sounds were obscene.

I'd had quite a few rim jobs in my life, all of them on set.

This? Nothing compared to this.

"Hugh. I'll come. You'll make me come."

He squeezed my cock, pumping fast, and shoved his tongue deeper while sucking on my hole.

I ground my ass against his mouth, and he held me tighter as if he wanted to suck me dry. My orgasm made me wail, overwhelming and not enough at the same time. My cock sprayed cum all over my torso and slick poured out of my spasming hole, but my insides ached with emptiness.

Hugh's loud groans and gulps resonated into me, prolonging my climax until I was shuddering.

Two seconds later, he was on top of me, his mouth on mine. I savored the taste of my slick on his lips and tongue. He made me taste delicious.

Huge and firm, his cockhead slid over my drenched, tingling rim. Without hesitation, I reached for his cock and guided it inside me.

The moan he let out sounded almost painful.

My flesh gave way easily, swallowing him up, the tissue eager for the exquisite friction. He wasn't the longest I'd had, but it was more than enough and *thick*. So fucking thick and firm. Like all of him. Meaty, big, hard, all over me and inside me, strong muscles, and the sharp tang of alpha musk... The round head glided deeper, stretching my insides, and deeper still, and I clutched at Hugh's shoulders, exhilarated.

This was it.

The perfect cock.

"Yes. I love it. Give me all of it. Give it to me. Please, Hugh. Fuck me hard. Fuck me with your beautiful cock. Love your fat cock, put it all the way, deeper, deeper..." *Oh shit.* I was saying it all out loud. *Fuck.*

"I've got you. I'll give you anything you want."

And he thrust.

Hard.

My lower body exploded in tingles, my guts singing with joy. Hugh pushed his ramrod-straight, fat dick into me to the hilt, over and over, and I melted into a puddle of goo.

"So wet. You're so wet and open for me. You've wanted me too. Admit it. You've wanted me all this time just like I've wanted you."

"Yes. Always."

"Fuck, Kirby."

And he kissed me. His cock dug into me, his tongue tangled with mine, and I came again. I'd been starving for this man, and now when the floodgates opened, I couldn't get enough. Hugh smeared my cum over my torso, rubbing it into my belly and nipples, and his smug smile made me want to bite him.

When the orgasm abated, I pushed on his shoulders, and he understood, rising and bringing me with him. He sat up, and I straddled his hips. I bounced up and down, searching for the best angle, then I leaned back, and his cockhead finally hit the mouth to my womb. It created the best sensation, a promise of a deep, messy breeding, and I shouted my joy. Another climax rushed through me, and I ground down, feeding it. *He'll breed me. This man will breed me.*

Hugh dug his fingers into my hips and gazed up at me, his features warped with want. He looked as if he were angry, but I knew better.

"Come inside me. Fuck your cum deep into me."

Snarling, he flipped us again, throwing me around like a rag doll. I ended up on my back, my ass hanging off the sofa, and he knelt on one knee, pulling me onto his dick with ruthless force.

I was already so fucked out he could have fisted me and my body would've just sighed with gratitude. He gave me long, firm thrusts, sliding slowly out, root to tip, and slamming back in. I didn't know whether I was still coming or not. I was probably already overstimulated but so damned happy I purred.

Hugh, damn him, gripped my throat. "Look at me," he ordered. Of course, I obeyed. I'd do anything he asked.

Drowning in pleasure, I watched him lose his control. What a glorious sight.

His look changed from aggressive intensity into tender awe and then bliss. Groaning, he nestled himself deep in my bruised flesh, as deep as he could, and I could feel his cock pulsate against the sealed mouth to my womb.

Then he bent down and kissed me. Circling his hips, stirring the cum and slick inside me, he kissed me for ages. He nipped at my swollen lips, suckled on my tongue, and delved in and out of my mouth when I tried to capture him. He bit me teasingly, then licked my lower lip to soothe it. All the time, he kept us joined.

"We're so doing this, Kirby. You're not getting out now."

"I don't want to get out of it."

"Good. Because this hole is mine. And I'm going to breed you so well."

"You're still hard." Did he need more? Because I'd give him more.

"Uh-huh. Are you sore?"

"Not really, but I want to suck you."

Carefully, he pulled out and kissed my temple. "I'd love that." Hissing, he squeezed his shaft in his hand. I wanted to worship that cock.

"Sit back."

When I got on my knees between his spread legs, Hugh looked at me like I was some deity.

Finally, I had it in front of me in real life. This man's gorgeous cock, covered with slick and cum, rising proudly right in front of my face.

I leaned in and kissed the slit.

CHAPTER 5

HUGH

Unbelievable.

I was panting, my pulse racing, skin prickling. Even though I'd already come, my erection reared between my legs like a flagpole.

And Kirby grinned up at me.

With the tip of his tongue, he traced a smear of cum on the side of my shaft, then licked his lips.

"Your dick is a work of art, Hugh."

My chuckle died when Kirby dragged his tongue up the underside and then smoothly took my entire cock down his throat. His stretched lips tightened around the base.

"Fuck!"

I managed not to buck, but a tremor ran through me. Kirby bobbed his head, doing something mind-blowing with his tongue around my crown before he sucked me to the root again. How the hell did he do that? For a split second, it occurred to me that *the* Kirby Matthews, the country's wettest dream, was sucking my cock. But that egotistical thought gave way to another, way more important and overwhelming one.

My Kirby. My omega.

I weaved my fingers through his hair and made myself relax into the sofa. Closing my eyes, I focused on the warmth of his mouth, the teasing hint of teeth, and the wicked tongue swirling over my most sensitive skin. My balls were already tight anew. His throat convulsed around my cockhead, and he pulled away for a deep breath. Then he dove down again, and again, until he just moved his head up and down a fraction, letting my cock slide through his open throat. My eyes popped open wide. Didn't he need to breathe?

Apparently not.

Involuntarily, I tightened my grip on his hair. "I'm close." Was that my voice?

Kirby's gaze flashed to mine, and I tried to hold it as he slid up my tingling cock and sucked the upper half while milking the base. With his other hand, he squeezed my balls gently.

The hunger in his eyes short-circuited my brain. I poured my cum into Kirby's magical mouth, giving him everything I had, until my balls ached with emptiness.

He swallowed it all, humming as if I'd fed him a treat. His eyelashes fluttering, he licked my cock like a cat, cleaning me root to tip. Then he kissed the crown all over until he gave one last suckling kiss to the slit, making me twitch with aftershocks.

Holy shit.

For some insane reason, he looked almost insecure when he peered up at me and wiped his mouth with the back of his hand. After what must have been the single most glorious blowjob in the history of blowjobs, Kirby bit his lip and his eyebrows scrunched up. My need to reassure him was immediate and powerful.

"Come here, little kitten."

I offered him my hands and brought him up so he straddled my lap. On instinct, my hand dove between his ass cheeks. I covered his opening with my finger, smearing around the cum that had leaked out, massaging it into his skin.

"You're incredible. You've blown my mind."

A corner of his mouth lifted at the praise.

"Kiss me, Kirby."

He leaned down and nipped at my upper lip. I opened my mouth to welcome him in while I slid a finger into his sloppy hole. Full of my cum and his slick. So much slick. Because I'd fucked him through at least three orgasms.

"This okay?" I checked.

"Yeah," he breathed before deepening the kiss.

I fingerfucked him while we explored each other's mouths for long minutes. Adding a second and then a third finger, I slowly brought him higher.

"You'll give me your beautiful hole? Let me knot you and breed you?"

"Uh-huh. Anything you want."

"Such a beautiful, warm hole, so fucking wet. I can't wait for your heat so I can put my whole fist in you. Will it make you come?"

"Yes. Fuck yes."

"Do you hear yourself, darling? Purring. Mmm. You like this, don't you?" I curled my fingers, pumping harder, and Kirby made *that* sound again. "Happy kitty. That's it. I'm going to keep your hole stuffed."

I changed back to two but added my other hand so I could stretch his opening with my fingers.

"Fuuuck! Fuck, Hugh. Yes. Like that. Stretch me out."

Four. I pumped four fingers, two from each hand, deep into him, and his slick poured out, dripping on my thighs. He fumbled for his cock and stroked it with a little twist around the crown. I was cataloging every detail so I could bring him even more pleasure next time.

"Hugh... I'm... Oh God!"

"I'll fuck you with my knot. Breed you over and over."

He came with his face tucked in the crook of my shoulder, whimpering softly, and I kept my fingers in him, holding him to me like that. I didn't want to break the connection between us. Not now, and not ever.

Kirby shivered, impaled on four fingers, his breathing harsh, but he didn't make a move to dislodge me. I kissed him again.

He was so pliant, open wide. He seemed so eager to please me. Like a good little omega. Like he was really giving himself to me, letting me do whatever I wanted with him.

The subtle whooshing of the elevator behind the walls reminded me of the outside world way too soon. Gently removing my fingers from Kirby's perfect body, I broke the kiss.

"I need to go. I promised my nephew and brother I'd be at home."

Kirby leaned his forehead against mine. "Okay." He'd tensed again.

"Don't avoid me, please."

"Not like I can anymore. Brian wants to do the trial on Tuesday, and my heat will come over the next weekend."

"I know. It'll be okay."

"Yeah."

I brought my wet fingers to my mouth for the last taste of his essence.

"I don't want to stop touching you, but I really must go."

On a sigh, Kirby threw his leg over my lap and stood. I admired his naked body as he walked through the living area toward the sleek granite kitchen counter on the other side of the open floor plan. He poured himself a glass of water and gulped it down.

He looked like a fae with his long legs, small, perky butt, and the smooth lines of his torso. Kirby possessed both raw sex appeal and elegant grace. I vividly remembered his catlike dark eyes and swollen lips on those posters downtown. No wonder his modeling career was picking up; Kirby was mesmerizing, his entire being so erotic, with a magnetic pull worthy of a siren.

I ate up his naked form, those glorious planes of smooth skin I'd kiss all over. The smears of slick on his ass cheeks and thighs glistened... Kirby glanced at me, tilting his head to the side.

"Weren't you leaving?"

"Shit. Yeah."

He handed me a paper towel to clean up the worst of the mess on my stomach. Then I dragged my T-shirt over my head and pulled my underwear back on. Kirby didn't bother to dress. Was he doing it on purpose? If so, it was working. Watching him walk around his apartment stark naked, red blotches of skin showing where I'd gripped him tight, I couldn't wait to fuck him again.

Except next time, we wouldn't be alone.

Dressed, I approached him carefully. Would he put distance between us again?

"Did it help?" I asked.

He snorted a startled laugh. "What?"

"The fucking. Did it help with the nerves?"

He gnawed on his lip, looking away. "Hugh. I don't even know where to start..."

Running my hand up his arm, I stepped closer. "We're good together, Kirby. We click. We both felt it before, and this just confirmed it. It's going to be great, right?"

He nodded, not meeting my gaze. What was bugging him?

I cupped his jaw and brought his face up so he'd look at me. The flash of vulnerability in his eyes made my knees weak. "What's wrong?"

"Nothing. It's going to be great."

Would he ever trust me enough to be honest with me?

I wouldn't push now. I had put us into this situation, but I wouldn't regret it. The thought of Kirby spending the heat with someone else, professional or not, made bile rise into my throat. No. Kirby was mine now. I leaned in, kissed him, and he let me in easily. Breathing him in, savoring the scent of recent orgasms and a little bit of sweat, I squeezed him tight.

"Do you want us to see each other before next week? I'm working every day because Derek is covering for me during the filming, but you can come to the pub. I'd love to see you." I knew what he'd say, but I wanted to let him know my wishes.

"I have stuff...work to do. I'll see you on the set on Tuesday."

Yep. I'd known, but it still hurt. "Okay." One last kiss. "Goodnight, Kirby."

"Night."

He didn't even look at me.

The night was chilly, so I decided to jog home, hoping it

would clear my head. Except running had the undesirable effect of letting me think and fantasize without distraction.

Kirby's face when he came, the sight of his open hole, the feeling of his stretched rim around my fingers, the taste of his slick... And me being more of a protective and caring alpha... Well, I was. But when it came to Kirby, I was getting possessive as hell.

My entire being chanted *mine mine mine* when I fucked him.

Brian had said that Kirby didn't have anything scheduled this month so he'd rest before the heat. Meaning he wasn't fucking anyone on camera but me.

But he was still a porn star. That was his job. And I used to tell myself I didn't care what he did because I wanted him and not just his body. I'd thought I'd been so noble and progressive.

Until today.

After bringing him pleasure, coming inside him, into his ass and mouth, my alpha claimed him as mine. As if the one fuck erased all sex partners either of us had had before, and now we belonged to each other. We were tied to each other, and the heat would only solidify our bond.

Such archaic nonsense.

Kirby didn't belong to anyone, and my alpha was a primitive oaf.

CHAPTER 6

KIRBY

"I slept with Hugh."

Emerson stopped in his tracks and pinned his huge eyes on me. Bo made a discontented noise in his carrier tied to Emerson's chest, so Emerson took the baby's hands and resumed walking slowly down the path, bouncing on his feet.

"I heard that right. You said you had sex with Hugh."

"That's what I said."

"Hm." My friend looked away, pretending to watch a passing jogger, but his mind was going a hundred miles an hour. I knew him better than myself sometimes. "And was it good?"

Good didn't even cover half of it. "Phenomenal."

"Oookay," Emerson drawled quietly.

I couldn't tell Emerson about the project. I'd be breaking the NDA. Not that Emerson would ever pass it on, but accidents happened, and if he let it slip, my career would be in danger.

"It's a big deal, isn't it?" he asked, still acting disinterested, which must have cost him a lot. I guessed the baby plastered to his torso was the only thing stopping him from jumping up and down and yelling.

"Not really," I replied in the same tone. *Liar, liar, pants on fire.*

"He's the first guy you've had sex with who isn't a client or a coworker."

"Since I was a teen, yeah." It was a bit of a gray zone, but technically... He was definitely the first I couldn't resist even though all my instincts told me it was a bad idea. "I'm a bit scared."

"Of Hugh? Why? He wouldn't hurt you."

"Not of *him*. I mean, he is...intense, but he's the definition of harmless, right? I once saw a guy spit in his face, and Hugh just wordlessly dragged him out of the pub and closed the door. I'd have punched the fucker. It's just that he's already a part of my life. I don't know how it'll affect us all."

"Depends."

"On what?"

Emerson shrugged, rubbing the baby's tiny palms with his thumbs. Bo was asleep now, his little face peeking out of the fleece hoodie, eyes closed, chubby cheeks glowing pink.

"Do you want to do it again? Does he? Are you dating?"

"Fuck no."

Emerson seemed to start at my sudden outburst. "Shh. You'll wake him up."

"Sorry."

"Why is that such a big no-no for you?"

"How can't you and Burke ever get this into your

heads? I sleep with people for a living. I can't just randomly date."

"Of course you can. Does Hugh mind?"

"No idea. We haven't talked about it."

"Never?"

"Well, once, we hinted at the possibility, but I shut it down before it could become anything."

Emerson's face split into a gleeful grin. "So he did hit on you in the past. I've wondered."

"Only once, and we weren't sober."

"Were you drunk this time?"

"No."

"What changed?"

How could I have had a reasonable conversation about my dilemma with Emerson without telling him the NDA stuff? I ignored his question.

"I don't want to lose a friend, Emerson. And he's close to Burke. To you. If it goes to hell—"

"Hugh's not that petty. He likes you a lot and never made a secret of it. I've wondered if you'd ever give him a chance. Honestly, I'm a bit excited right now."

I was too. Which was a part of why I was freaking out. "I like him too."

"That's awesome, Kirby!" Emerson squealed before biting his lip. He hugged the baby protectively and pulled the fleece to the side to check. Bo was still out for the count. "Does he want to keep seeing you?" my friend asked in a low voice.

"We shouldn't. It would never work." *Definitely not outside work.*

"That's why you've been avoiding him."

"You noticed?"

"Everybody did. Hugh seemed sad about it."

"Fuck. See? It's already going downhill."

"But that was before you slept together."

"Um." The conversation wasn't helping my confused state at all.

"I don't get it, Kirby. What's really going on with you and Hugh? Are you like in love but can't be together because you do porn? Because that's ridiculous. I'm sure if you'd just talk about it..."

I snorted. The word 'love' always brought my sarcastic side out to play. "I've slept with hundreds of guys, Emerson. Hundreds of dicks, gallons of cum, years and years of wet ass and sore throat, and it was only recently I started really enjoying it. Access to a shower after a fuck makes a helluva difference. And honestly, I don't need much more than that to have a good time." Emerson scoffed, about to protest, but I ignored it. "I can't expect an alpha to willingly share my body with others. Not that anybody ever wanted me that way. For most people, I'm hot meat with holes to plow into, and that's okay. I like it. I get off on it. It pays for my apartment, these nice clothes, long lazy showers, and all the cheese I want. I don't want it to change. I like being everybody's whore. I'm good at it."

My friend stopped and turned to face me. He had his determined face on, and I was once again grateful for the baby he wore. It meant he couldn't fight me or yell at me. "You just told me you have feelings for Hugh."

"I haven't said anything like that."

"You told me you slept with him and that you're now afraid."

I threw my arms into the air, exasperated. "Of messing up. Losing him as a friend. Losing Burke, and you."

Emerson glared. "You'll never lose us."

"Even if it gets messy between Hugh and me?"

"Will it?"

"I don't know!"

"Well, I can't see what horrible thing you'd have to do to push us all out of your life."

"Considering I'm a whore and a thief, that means a lot. Thank you, Em."

My friend grimaced. "Please, don't use those words to describe yourself. And it wouldn't be the end of the world to let yourself feel something for an alpha, you know."

"Every alpha is either a client or a problem." I repeated our old mantra, winking at him, and finally, Emerson smiled.

"Burke isn't," he said softly.

"Well, Hugh *is* a problem at the moment."

"I like Hugh. He's a great guy. The way he takes care of his little brother and Monty... And have you seen him with Bo?"

I had. I wrinkled my nose. Kids didn't do it for me. "If you say so."

"When's the big filming?"

I had to pause in my head to remind myself that Emerson had changed the subject and didn't know about Hugh and me filming together. "Next weekend. I'll go into heat around Saturday."

"But then you'll be done before Christmas, right? I thought you'd spend Christmas Day with us."

"Sorry, Em, but I'll probably still be recovering. I'll let you know, okay? I'll be with you on New Year's in any case." Christmas was just another day for me. I usually stayed away from all the fuss. The New Year's parties at Burke's were becoming a tradition, though.

"Okay." Emerson sounded disappointed but wouldn't push. "Are you, um, excited about filming the heat again?"

"Yes," I answered truthfully. "And nervous."

"The alpha that Brian chose, do you like him? Is he okay?"

"He's interesting."

If Emerson only knew.

BRIAN TOLD me to dress however I wanted but go for contrasts. Hugh was a big guy, rough around the edges, with intricate tattoos sprawling up his arms and back, light body hair and tanned skin. So my stylist and I chose a black long-sleeved top, sheer and shimmery, and tight like a second skin. We matched it with black lace briefs and see-through white pants. Eyeliner, lip gloss. No point in putting any product into my hair since I'd be rolling around on a bed.

The walk down the hallway to the fake bedroom seemed endless. My heart pounded in my throat. Had I ever been this nervous before a shoot? Not since my first, no.

Hugh was sitting on the bed, talking to Brian who stood in front of him. They both turned to me when I entered. The awkwardness was instant and heavy.

"Hi, Kirby. You look fabulous!" Brian's enthusiasm fell flat. He glanced from Hugh to me and back. "Well—"

"Hi." Hugh stood and took a couple of steps toward me. He eyed me as if I was about to bite him.

Fuck.

"Hi," I replied lamely.

Then the man did something that made my brain go completely blank. He hugged me and kissed my cheek softly. "You okay, kitten?" he whispered.

My reply came on autopilot. "Uh-huh. You?"

"Yeah. I'm fine. You look beautiful." He ran his fingers down the side of my face.

"Thanks."

He'd trimmed his beard to a short stubble, and his head was freshly shaved. He wore a simple white shirt and jeans and was barefoot. I inhaled his delicious scent. No perfume or aftershave, just clean, warm skin and hints of alpha musk. His blue eyes roamed my face, and one corner of his mouth lifted into a soft smirk.

"Erm." Brian's unsubtle clearing of his throat broke the moment.

I took a step back, but Hugh kept us connected, sliding his hand down my arm and holding my wrist in a light grip. What was he doing? This was work, not a date. And why was I letting him?

"We double-checked the lighting with stand-ins and then with Hugh since he was here early. Remember, this is a trial run, so no pressure, but if something looks good, we'll use it in the final cut and bonus material. You've both read my notes, I presume?"

Hugh and I nodded. Brian didn't do proper scripts, claiming it only made performers do the kind of acting they sucked at. He always gave me rough descriptions of what he expected of each scene, which worked fine for me. I liked to freestyle.

"Great." Brian rubbed his hands together like he always did right before a shoot. It made him look like a cartoon villain.

The technician and cameraman did their magic rituals and exchanged words in code I never understood. Brian wanted as few people in the room as possible, so another couple of guys whom I'd noticed fiddling with the lights and cables when I'd come in now left, closing the double door behind them.

Brian settled into his chair.

"We're good to go."

I wasn't. I'd read the notes and forbidden myself to overthink it. I'd thought I'd just wing it.

But now when I stood here, facing Hugh, I was frozen in place.

Scene 1 in front of the bed.

Slow touches over clothing. Exploratory.

Close-ups on hands, neck, ass. Kissing.

Intimate, affectionate. Focused.

Hugh bit his lip, inched closer, and searched my gaze. What was he looking for? My permission? That was implied.

He touched my hand, and I realized it was closed in a fist. On a deep exhale, I released it, and he stroked my fingers before massaging the center of my palm with his thumb.

I was brilliant at this. Sex was what I excelled at, straight As, five stars, flying colors. There was no need for me to be nervous.

"Hey, kitten, it's okay," he whispered so quietly I barely heard it. "It's just me."

That was the problem, though. Didn't he get it? It was *him*, and not just anyone.

He shuffled closer still and cupped my jaw with his other hand. Rubbed my lips with his thumb. His breath fanned my face.

"Close your eyes, Kirby."

I obeyed. The lights were gone, the subtle movements of the crew in my peripheral vision, the dust circling in the air…gone.

Hugh's nose brushed mine. A tickle of his beard. Another hot breath, this time so close, it felt like a touch. I parted my lips in expectation. The taste of his kisses was fresh in my memory, just like the taste of his cum. I wanted both. I'd get both again.

When he finally kissed me, I was ready. I opened for him, meeting him halfway, sliding my tongue against his. He ran his hands down my back and squeezed my ass cheeks, pulling me close. Fuck, he was huge. The mountain of a man surrounded me, all warm, strong, and steady, and I softened in his thick arms, my tension disappearing. Hugh massaged my ass cheeks with his powerful hands, and his hard cock dug into my underbelly. He rubbed up and down my crease through the fabric, and I sensed the camera somewhere close, the extra presence a familiar comfort. The room was quiet besides my gasps and Hugh's soft grunts.

I was wet and open already, and judging by how Hugh deepened the filthy kiss, he must have smelled it.

Smoothing my hands over his shoulders and pecs, I got impatient. I wanted skin. Button after button, I opened his shirt while he grazed my neck with his teeth and nibbled on the tendons there. When I got rid of the annoying shirt, I barely had time to take in his gorgeous torso before he sank down. He nuzzled my stomach and lifted my top to expose my belly button. Pushing the tip of his tongue into it, he fisted my pants by my hips and pulled them down, revealing my skimpy briefs. Grinning, he bit the edge of the black lace. He liked them, I could tell.

I stepped out of my pants and moaned when Hugh mouthed my erection through the see-through underwear. His hands went back to my ass, tracing the lines of the briefs and skimming along my crease.

My hole let out a trickle of slick, wetting the pretty briefs. I didn't usually get wet this much this fast, definitely not on set. It could have been the upcoming heat...or Hugh.

He stood, dragging my top over my head in one smooth movement. The next second, his mouth was on my nipple.

My chest was sensitive, especially close to heat, and today, my nipples were aching, hard and red, itching for attention. He nibbled and kissed them, suckled gently, but that wasn't what I needed.

"Harder," I gasped. "Bite them."

Hugh's eyes lit up with a dangerous fire. He drew my nipple into his mouth and sucked hard, painfully so, then he clamped down on it with his teeth.

I moaned, my head falling back. The pain shot from my nipple right into my balls and hole, and I shivered with delight. Hugh sucked and bit the other one, and I pushed my chest into his face for more. He was pinching and tugging on them, biting them and licking to soothe them before biting even harder. My hole gushed slick like a broken pipe.

"Hand, Kirby." Brian's voice. I'd forgotten about him. And true enough, I was holding Hugh's head with my left hand, hiding his face from the camera. I dropped my arm and grabbed Hugh's nape with my right hand.

The interruption helped, though. It allowed me to slow down and refocus.

Hugh kissed my nipples tenderly as if saying sorry for abusing them so harshly before.

"Bed," Brian said.

Hugh sat with his legs spread, leaning back, and I attacked his jeans. He had nothing underneath, clever man. His cock reared in front of my face, and in the studio lighting, it looked truly magnificent. Massive, fat, veiny, with a bulging head, the foreskin pulled back a little exposing the glistening, sensitive skin at the tip—a fucking king of dicks. I kissed the base and ran my nose along the length, pulling in the distinct alpha scent. How had I ever doubted this? Having Hugh spread out for me like a delicious meal was brilliant.

By this point, my briefs were drenched. Once I went into heat, we wouldn't have time to explore, so I needed to make the best of this. I suckled the head, savoring the fullness in my mouth, imagining how it would feel sliding into my horny hole. Mmm, perfect.

Did I purr?

Hugh smiled at me and tangled his fingers in my hair.

"Hungry kitty," he mouthed, smirking.

It was true. I was ravenous for his dick.

Taking it down my throat, I let the pleasure course through me. When I could control it, I liked deepthroating. Loved it. Almost as much as fucking. Well, no, that was probably a lie. Nothing compared to a proper fucking. But having a dick lodged deep in my throat was a close second. I bobbed my head, and Hugh's fist tightened in my hair. He pushed gently, and I took him in until my lips touched his pubes. Fuck, the girth. I couldn't breathe, but my whore brain took it as just another layer of lust. I relished the stretch, the helplessness, the edge of danger. Salt and musk and hot, hard meat... My stomach clenched with hunger, and I retreated only to plunge down again faster, letting the big cock spear my throat. *Yes. Fuck yes.*

Brian had said this was a trial run, right? So I didn't have to focus all the time.

Hugh's thighs trembled, his body tense, and his grunts got increasingly louder. *Good.*

"Stop," he ordered.

Somewhat disappointed, I retreated. I kissed his cock-head goodbye, sat on my haunches, and waited for him to tell me what he wanted me to do next.

I gazed up at him, motionless.

Hugh pushed his thumb between my lips, and I suckled on it.

I'm waiting for his order. Like an obedient little omega.

He fucked my mouth with his finger, then grabbed my throat, tugging me up from the floor. With one swift movement, he toppled me onto the bed next to him and all but tore my briefs off.

He ran his hand up my thigh, over my waist, and to my nipple. He pinched it and watched my cock twitch in response. Then he tugged on my hip, and I rolled onto my knees. His fingers traced my asshole.

"You're gorgeous."

I couldn't remember ever being this horny. Something in my head felt off, like I was a little drunk even though I hadn't had any alcohol in days. But I was too keyed up to worry about it. All that mattered was the emptiness in my ass and the anticipation of a good, thorough fuck.

Wiggling, I bowed my spine, stretching like a cat, waving my ass in the air. I wasn't even doing it for the camera. It was all for Hugh. He liked seeing me like this, wet and open for him, aching for his cock. And I wanted to please him—which was best done on my knees, ass up.

Like a good little omega.

CHAPTER 7

HUGH

Kirby's pink hole looked absolutely stunning. The wide gape was now at least half-an-inch, the skin around it glistening with all the slick he'd leaked. In this position, with the lights aimed at him, I could even glimpse the raw flesh inside.

I cupped those round muscles and placed a slow kiss just above his perfect little opening.

Kirby stretched again, rocking his hips and curving his spine, and I rewarded him with a flick of my tongue over his rim.

"Please." His voice was just a meek whimper. My darling boy needed me.

Impatient to taste his slick properly, I shoved my tongue into the soft hole. God, he was open like a highway, no resistance at all, just silky flesh, heat, and an abundance of juices. Sweet and thick like honey.

"Aaah. Mmm. Yeah. Lick me deep. Please. Kiss my hole. Kiss my filthy hole... Need it. Need you."

His pleading cries went straight to my cock. I burrowed as deep as I could, sucking and swallowing, wiggling my tongue and shoving it in and out.

"Coming!"

I heard a shuffle and a thump as the cameraman must have moved to get a cum shot, but I ignored him.

Kirby keened, pushing his ass into my face. His hole spasmed and fluttered, and I licked him through the orgasm while he sprayed the sheets with his cum.

Slowly, I kissed the twitching hole until Kirby stopped shuddering.

"Your cock," he gasped.

I stood and lined up. I half expected Brian to say something, but the room was quiet except for Kirby's needy whimpers.

Kirby's rim clamped onto my cockhead, hot, tight, loving... Our surroundings dissolved into thin air. It was just Kirby and me, and an invisible crowd of strangers admiring us from afar, aching but unable to touch us. They all envied me, hundreds and thousands of horny alphas, staring at my gorgeous omega, at his eager hole, wishing they could be me... But they couldn't have my boy. Kirby was mine.

My cockhead slid deeper inside him, and I gently fucked the wide gape with it, watching it loosen even more. Oily slick was pouring out, smearing my cock and hand and dripping down Kirby's balls. Kirby's moans got high-pitched and needy. So gloriously horny. He was close to his heat—that must have been the reason. But fuck, it was hotter than the lowest circles of hell.

I couldn't wait anymore. With very little thought to camera angles, I pushed and sheathed myself in Kirby's body to the hilt.

"Fuck yes!" he cried and rocked back, chasing me when I tried to retreat.

I gripped his hips tight and thrust in and out a couple of times, holding him firmly in place. Humming, he relaxed into my hold, letting me set the pace.

"There. I'll take care of you. My needy little kitten."

I gave him long strokes, filling him up, teasing his closed womb with my cockhead. His sweet purrs turned into loud groans of pleasure, guttural and animalistic.

He came around my cock after barely a minute, shaking, and his hole released another river of slick. I scooped up a few drops and licked them from my fingers. Like fucking manna.

Another climax.

"Good boy. That's it. Come on my dick."

Then I remembered we weren't alone.

I manhandled Kirby around until he sat in my lap facing the main camera. He was limp in my arms, jolting with my thrusts, his head lolling on my shoulder. I gripped his erection and milked it while I pumped my hips faster. I loved him like this, helpless and all soft, open and welcoming. Three lenses were pinned on his spread-out body, witnessing his pleasure. Kirby kept coming, his hole pulsating in waves, and I wanted to roar with victory. *He loves how I fuck him, and after this, everybody will know.*

I was on the edge, but I could hold it a while longer. I wouldn't have applied for this job if I didn't know how to keep myself under control.

Kirby keened with another release, shuddering head to toe. When his cries quieted, his body turned to jelly, his moans exhausted, I relented. I pulled him off my cock and shoved him down onto his knees by the bed. Gripping his hair, I held his face up as I stood above him.

He looked wrecked. Sweaty, face blotched with red, lips bitten, tears in his eyes. *Wrecked*.

Peering up at me through his lashes, his expression dazed with lust, he opened his mouth obediently. A hungry whine escaped from his throat. And the sound, fuck, it went straight to my balls. My hand flying over my slick erection, I painted his lips and tongue with cum. I'd saved up for this moment. Yes, that was how vain I was. I hadn't come in four days, waiting for this, and now I gave it all to Kirby, the load of the year, of my fucking lifetime. My cock spurted thick cream in four, five, six doses, and Kirby ate it like a baby bird. He licked his lips and sucked my cockhead into his mouth, humming contentedly. His eyes closed, he suckled on the slit. His face seemed blank, as if he were dreaming. As if the sex brought him into some kind of trance. The sight made all my protective instincts rise. He was defenseless like this, trusting and eager to please, and he needed me.

I got down on the floor and caught his face between my hands. Kissing him deep, I tasted my cum and his slick, and it was heavenly. With a moan, Kirby scampered into my lap, and I held him to me, deepening the kiss. He clung to me, and I never wanted the moment to end.

We leaned against the mattress from our spot on the floor and made out, sticky with drying bodily fluids. I pushed my finger into his hole, just to stroke it goodbye, and my kitten purred.

His movements slowed; he must have been tired, so I slowly pulled out of his ass and gave it a gentle pat. Kirby smiled against my lips.

Breaking the kiss, I looked him over. His lips were swollen, eyelids drooping, unguarded gaze pinned on me like he was waiting for me to give him another order that he'd readily obey. He looked so soft, meek even.

My Kirby.

I opened my mouth to say—

"Excellent. That was amazing, guys. Thank you."

Brian.

The shutters closed in Kirby's eyes, and his expression fell. He stood in one languid movement, and before I could comprehend what was happening, he had a white terrycloth robe wrapped around his body.

"I'm going to shower," he said to no one specific. With that, he left the room.

I was still kneeling on the floor by the bed, wet dick out and mouth agape.

CHAPTER 8

KIRBY

My stomach felt iffy again. Even after a long shower, half an hour on the treadmill, and another shower, I was coming out of my skin. I once read somewhere that views had a calming effect on people, that focusing your eyes on the far distance activated some part of your brain that told you to chill. Well, my spectacular view over the ocean wasn't doing shit for me today.

Fingers shaking, I typed a message to Brian.

Me: *I need to talk to Sébastien before the heat. I'll pay myself but need your help to get a time slot. I don't even have his contact info, and his website only lists the email address to his PA.*

Brian: *Are you okay? Sure, I'll message him immediately.*

Me: *I'm fine. Just overly cautious. Nothing that will affect the production.*

In two minutes, my phone rang.

"I said I was fine, Brian. I'll be ready to go on Friday."

"I'm not worried about the production."

I snorted at that. *Yeah, right.*

"Okay. Not only about the production. Are you sure you're okay? You left abruptly. Today was truly impressive, Kirby. Hugh is great, and you two seem to be exceptionally compatible. Cameron was bitching about angles and the lack of close-ups when you left, but in my opinion, that's a minor issue. I'm extremely happy with this pairing." In true Brian fashion, he went off down his own lane, not even waiting for me to reply. "I already messaged Walter, and he got back immediately that he'd call you. I only need to send him your number. I really hope you're satisfied with today's shooting. You were brilliant. And the finale on your face. You should have seen yourself. You looked high on sex."

He was not helping my freakout.

"Can you send my number to Walter?"

"Already done. I have my earphones in. I can't take calls without them anymore. It annoys me not to be able to use both hands. I should probably let you go in case Walter calls."

"Thank you, Brian."

"Lovely. Take care, Kirby, rest, and I'll see you on Friday?"

"Sure. Have a nice evening, Brian."

"You too, superstar."

I took a deep breath and a gulp of my drink. The chilly breeze blew right through my hoodie, and I got a flashback to a night on a cardboard bed down behind the train tracks in East Village. I pushed off the railing and went back into my apartment, closing the balcony door firmly behind me. Impatient, I checked the screen as if I could summon Walter Sébastien by staring at it.

As if he could help.

Well, if not him, then no one could.

Luckily, Walter had time for me the following evening. I had to visit him at home, though, since it was after his usual hours. I was fully aware and grateful he made an exception for me.

The house was really nice, newly renovated, with a small garden and big maple trees looming above the short driveway. A neat family home. Even before I knocked, a dog began barking behind the door.

"Rusty, sit. Sit, you maniac."

Walter opened the door and smiled at me.

"Hi, Kirby."

Aside from the rather large, reddish canine that sat behind him and stared at me with tongue lolling out and tail thumping on the floor, a kid who-knew-how-old stood by Walter's side, holding on to his arm.

"Hi," I said.

"Sorry, Kirby. My husband is on his way home. As soon as he arrives, we can go to my study."

"That's fine. I'm really grateful you could see me at such short notice. Sorry to barge into your home."

"You're most welcome."

Suddenly, the dog shot out like a rocket and ran past me. Was I supposed to stop the animal? How?

"Oh shit," I muttered and spun around, half expecting to see a squirrel or a cat running for its life.

Instead, a short, bespectacled man walked up the driveway toward the house. The dog danced around the guy's feet, and the man petted it enthusiastically.

"Hello, Rusty. Lovely to see you too. Have you been guarding my boys?"

So this was the husband, I presumed. He looked rather unremarkable and clean-cut. Like an accountant or a lawyer. I didn't know why, but I had expected someone a bit edgier or something. But the look of pure adoration that spread over Walter's face said it all.

I stepped aside to give them space.

"Hi, love." Walter pulled his husband in for a kiss while the kid hugged his other dad around his waist.

The display of family bliss left me feeling a bit uncomfortable, but I remained quiet. After all, I was an intruder, not a guest.

"Guys, this is Kirby Matthews. Kirby, this is Teddy"—he pointed at the kid's head—"and this is my Daniel."

My lips twitched at the way he said 'my Daniel.' The great Walter Sébastien was whipped like cream.

"Hello, Kirby. So nice to meet you. Oh wow, you're just as beautiful in the flesh."

"Um. Hi. Sorry to impose this late."

"Not a problem. Walter said it was an emergency. It's me who's sorry. Parent meetings running late and then traffic. Teddy, have you eaten dinner?"

"Yeah," the kid said in a slightly annoyed tone.

"You're a teacher?" I asked as I followed them into the house, trying not to stumble over the wriggling pup. I would have petted him, but he moved way too fast, teeth and tongue everywhere. I wasn't sure it was wise to add my hand into that.

"Get off him, Rusty! Go lie down. Math and history. Can I offer you something to drink?"

It took me a second to sort through what Daniel meant by all of that. "I'm good, thank you. I really don't want to impose."

"Not imposing. Let's go to my office," Walter said.

Daniel kissed him again, on the lips, while the kid rolled his eyes theatrically and ran down the hallway toward an open space at the end. "Screen time," he screeched.

"Not for another fifteen minutes," Daniel yelled after him.

Lips twitching, Walter gestured for me to go to the left.

The office was a small room with dark paneling and a large window into the garden. Lamps illuminated the naked maple branches outside.

"You have a nice family," I said as he closed the door.

"I have no idea how you got that impression from the chaos, but I do, thank you. I'm very lucky in that aspect."

He sat in a low armchair, and I settled into the one opposite. "You sure you don't want anything to drink? Not even water?"

"Thanks, I'm good."

"So. What's the problem?"

"I'm about to go into heat. The doctor's exam says between Saturday and Monday, so I'm supposed to be on location starting Friday."

"Can I?" he gestured to my neck.

"Sure."

He sniffed at me and sat back down. "Saturday sounds about right. Any unusual symptoms?"

"No."

He looked thoughtful, squinting at me. "Do you want me to keep asking questions, or do you prefer to gather your thoughts and tell me yourself?"

"I'll...tell you."

He stapled his fingers on his stomach, looking at me neutrally. He was unnerving, and I didn't like baring my soul to anyone, let alone an arrogant, smug alpha like him. But he was also the man who'd helped me to understand my hang-ups before my last heat, and without him, I might still be smoking a joint before each filming. Yes, I used to do that. It made it easier for me to get aroused and orgasm during a shoot. Most omegas in the porn industry self-medicated in one way or another, and some producers happily provided the desired substances for free. Which often went to hell in *so* many ways. I'd gotten lucky. Walter had helped me to get into the right mindset, and Brian had made me feel safe. I could now enjoy sex entirely thanks to Walter Sébastien.

So I took a deep breath and talked. "We did the trial run two days ago. On Tuesday afternoon."

"Trial run?"

"Hugh and I had sex on camera for the first time."

Instead of asking a follow-up question, Walter waited, a mildly curious expression on his face.

"It went great. Brian was lyrical. But... Ugh." I rubbed my face. What the fuck was wrong with me? "I couldn't stay focused with Hugh. I got carried away. And it'll be even worse during heat."

Walter frowned. "Can you specify 'carried away'?"

"I got...into it. Forgot about the camera, about Brian and the crew."

"Did you enjoy the sex?"

I laughed humorlessly. "Fuck yeah."

"And Brian was happy with the session."

"Yes."

"You have to help me to see the problem. Correct me if I'm wrong, but isn't that just the type of authentic enjoyment that Brian wants to capture?"

"This was way more than enjoyment, Walter. It was like being high or drunk. I haven't lost control this way before."

"Not even during heat?"

"That was different. During heat, I was physically helpless, but aside from breeding orgasms, a part of me was always aware of my surroundings and what my task was. I was working."

"And on Tuesday you weren't."

"No. Once he was in me, I had no control over myself whatsoever. I think I almost passed out toward the end. And it's not even my heat yet. I didn't sense or care about anything but the alpha with me until Brian spoke up when we were done."

"Ah."

My eyes snapped up to his face at that one syllable. It sounded vaguely damning. "You understand what's going on?"

"There are several options. Heat cycles change with age. You're only twenty-seven, and some of your heats could still get stronger. For most people, the intensity starts ebbing first after forty or even forty-five. You could be experiencing a buildup before a strong heat."

"You said several options."

"You're comfortable with Brian, secure in your role, and can simply relax."

"No. That's not it. If anything, I was more nervous than

usual. But then I just...lost myself. I can't even describe it."

Walter studied me for a while. "Kirby, I remember you once told me you didn't really get the benefits of a live penis compared to a good dildo."

"I remember. A dildo doesn't come with a potential psycho attached to it and pulls out when you want it to."

"And that's why, even though you did enjoy intercourse, you preferred masturbation. I also remember you told me that filming porn made you feel safe during sex because there were other people present who could interfere in case the alpha you were with wanted to hurt you."

I looked away. The curtains had small snowflakes on them. Did the Sébastiens decorate for the holidays already? Well, it was barely a month away, and they had a kid... "The so-called trauma and all of that," I said. "Why are you bringing it up?"

"Kirby." I refocused on Walter. He raised his eyebrows at me and nodded as if I was supposed to get what he was about to say before he said it. "With Hugh, you let yourself be vulnerable during sex. That's amazing progress for you, don't you think?"

"No. I don't think losing control during a shoot is in any way progress."

Walter gave me a sour look. "You *do* want a life outside your work, don't you?"

I ignored the jab. "But why did it happen?"

"I think the most probable explanation would be that you trust Hugh Urban as a friend and that the two of you are sexually compatible."

I winced. I didn't like having it confirmed. I had hoped Walter would come up with some brilliant reasoning that wouldn't mean I was losing it because I was hooked on Hugh and his magical dick.

"How long have you known Hugh?" he asked.

"Three years, give or take. We've been friends for two."

"Have you ever had physical relations before Tuesday?"

"Um. Last weekend. I wanted to get it out of the way before the filming, and he agreed."

"Okay." He rubbed his chin and uncrossed his legs, leaning forward. "Was that intense as well?"

"Yeah, I guess. But Tuesday was insane."

"What's the worst that could happen?"

"That I fuck up on set."

Walter frowned, as if he didn't understand what I was saying. "Kirby, it's ten days. Some heat waves will be easier than others, but Brian will end up with hours of material to choose from for a ninety-minute movie. Hugh and Brian will be there to take care of you and help you through any crisis. I will be on the phone in case any heat-related issue appears, but you're healthy and it's not your first, so the chance is very low." He paused, waiting for me to look at him. "You came here for my opinion and advice. I'll ask you again, and you can choose to be honest with me so I can actually help you. What are you *really* afraid of?"

I closed my eyes and swallowed. When I reopened them, Walter was looking at me with a sad smile on his face. He already knew what the issue was. "That I'm developing feelings for Hugh."

"Thank you for trusting me. Brian would be over the moon to hear this, of course, but I'm not Brian. My task is to make sure you have a great, healthy heat."

"What's the advice then?"

"Don't ever tell Brian I said this, but I think you should back out of the project. You should spend your heat with Hugh alone and explore your mutual connection."

I scoffed. "Not in a million years. I have thousands of

fans waiting for this film. I can't back out and don't want to."

"Okay. So we're dealing with possible romantic attachment toward your coworker on set. And you're worried you won't be able to...perform like you're used to?"

"Yes."

"The loss of control, or let's call it loss of self-awareness. Was it unpleasant when it happened?"

I couldn't help but laugh. "I was too busy coming my brains out."

"So it got unpleasant after you *regained* control." The expression on his face was smug again, and I didn't like it.

"What if Hugh finds out?"

"Would that be so terrible?"

"I don't know. You tell me."

Walter blew out a breath. "Look, Daniel and I met under special circumstances. I thought it was impossible for us to be together. But it turned out that when you both want the same thing, all the other stuff ceases to matter."

"That's lovely, congratulations, but I'm not here for relationship advice. I need to pull off the most anticipated porn flick of the year."

"Is that what you care about the most?"

"Yes!" I cried, exasperated with his line of questioning.

He shrugged. "In that case, go lose control. It'll look spectacular on camera."

I threw him a glare.

"Kirby, I'm a heat consultant and a sex therapist. I'm not qualified to help you with your fear of attachment, but I really think you should talk to someone about it. I can give you the contact info for a couple of psychotherapists who might be a good match for you. But if you're worried about filming with Hugh because of the results, you don't have to. You were able to let go and lose yourself in the act already. I'd say, go enjoy it. Savor it. Talk to Hugh about your control issues so he can help you if you panic, but otherwise, I don't see a problem."

Fear of attachment. He was right, of course. The fucker.

I studied the snowflakes on the curtains again. They were tiny but detailed, with many different shapes and shades of blue. "What should I tell Hugh if I don't want to disclose the truth?"

"It's common that omegas enter an altered state of mind during a peaking heat. He should remain calm and soothe you. He shouldn't try waking you up from the trance, not with words and definitely not by slapping or shaking you or any of that nonsense. He should let it run its course. If he's read the material I've sent him, then he already knows."

"I'm sure he's read it."

"I still think you should tell him about your fears so he can take care of you in the best possible way. Or do you want me to talk to him instead?"

"No. I'll do it."

"Great."

It wasn't great at all.

"Kirby. This could be a good thing. For the filming, sure, but mostly for you. I like Hugh."

The words 'fear of attachment' rattled around my head as I made my excuses and thanked him. The session had calmed some of my panic, but a vague unease settled in my gut.

Walter, in his usual annoying manner, had pointed out what should have been obvious. I didn't have to worry about the movie. My wayward emotions, though? That shit was terrifying.

CHAPTER 9

HUGH

Okay, now I was getting annoyed. Just like Kirby had said —a lamb on a butcher's table. It was Friday afternoon, and Kirby was about to arrive, in good time before the first heat wave started, which Walter claimed would happen on Sunday morning at the latest. In the master bedroom on the second floor of Brian's summer house—which was the decided location for the filming—Cameron had me in his claws. Positions and angles all over again.

"You can't go on like you did on Tuesday, with your face stuck in his ass. I mean you can, but not for five minutes straight. And same with the fuck. I could barely see your dick going in." When Cameron got frustrated, his voice got squeaky. It was the most annoying thing I'd ever heard. I had a feeling he didn't like me much, and it was becoming mutual. "When you're doing him from behind, you bend over like this and make space between your legs. To get a close-up of the action, the camera's here. Get it?"

He adjusted my stance where I stood by the bed, braced

on my hands. Kirby was currently represented by a pillow. I felt vaguely humiliated.

"When the camera's here..." Cameron waited with his eyebrows raised, hands in the air as if holding an invisible box next to me. Did he want me to pose for him again like some dummy? We'd done this last week, and I'd hated it. I wouldn't be able to make love to Kirby, focus on his pleasure, and at the same time screw my body into a fucking spiral.

I straightened and crossed my arms over my chest. I'd had enough.

Seeing my expression, Cameron dropped his stance, rolling his eyes. "Dude, have you *seen* porn before? This is not a honeymoon. You fuck how we tell you, or there's ten guys waiting in line to take your place."

"Cameron," Brian said from the doorway, his tone ice-cold. "I think Hugh gets it."

The cameraman threw his hands in the air. "It's your movie, Brian. But don't complain you can't see shit when you hire an amateur himbo for your biggest project of the year." With that, he stormed out.

I gritted my teeth. And that guy was supposed to be here in the room with us while Kirby was in heat?

"I apologize, Hugh. I don't tolerate such behavior on set. I'll talk to him immediately." Brian's fingers flew over the screen of his phone as he said that. "It won't happen again."

I closed my eyes, trying to think around my anger. "I mean, he's right. I *am* an amateur."

Brian dropped his phone into his suit pocket and smiled. "And thank God for that. You and Kirby were the hottest thing I'd ever seen in a studio ever. Cameron needs to get more creative because I'm not messing with whatever you two have going on. Keep doing what you did on Tuesday, and it'll be perfect."

"What about the second cameraman?"

"Trent used to do reality shows. You know those where you lock people up in a house and film them twenty-four seven? He's here for the long shifts." Brian winked, and I grimaced. "He's as mellow as they come, and an omega as well. Sorry you couldn't meet him before, but he had another project up until last night on the East Coast. I'm grateful he can make it in time for Sunday."

I exhaled. "Okay. Sounds good."

"Anyway. You relax, and I'll deal with the crew. Are you and Kirby sharing the bedroom tonight or not?"

The non sequitur threw me. "We haven't talked about it."

"Oh. Well, the second bedroom across the hall is ready for you. There's no equipment. It's yours for the ten days, and Kirby will be staying here. He'll be glad to hear that the new bathroom has been fixed just in time. Want to have a look?"

He gestured to a discreet door to the left of the king-size bed, and I followed him. The shower stall was huge and open, the tiled floor space bigger than our kitchen at home. The counter held one wide sink and offered enough space for me to hoist Kirby up there and...

"We didn't have any bathroom action in the last heat film we made with Kirby. So this time I wanted possibilities."

Ah. All that floor space was for equipment and crew.

"But if I knot Kirby in here, then I have to get him to bed. It'll be uncomfortable for him."

"Aftercare, Hugh. I want to film the aftercare."

Now I felt stupid again. "Got it."

"Panic button here, same as next to the bed." He pointed at the small red button on the wall by the counter. "Kirby has been instructed to push it with the first sign of a heatwave coming. If he can't, you will. In the middle of the heat, the main camera might be on for most of the time in the bedroom even if no staff is present, so be aware of that. Cameron explained about the three-camera setup, I hope, before he stopped acting professional?"

"Yes. I even saw the diagrams. Two static, one in hand."

"Good." Brian walked out of the bathroom with a swish to his hips. He was bubbling with excitement on the inside, wasn't he? Or was he looking forward to chewing Cameron out?

In the bedroom, Kirby sat on the bed, typing on his phone. My heart fluttered at the sight of him. He was dressed in tight black jeans, an oversized hoodie, and a long black coat. By his feet lay a large duffel. Judging by the wetness in his hair, it was raining outside. Or maybe snowing?

"Hi," I said.

Kirby finished whatever he was typing and threw the phone onto the bed covers.

"Hi." He met my gaze briefly before looking at Brian. He was distancing himself again. *Dammit.*

"I'm knackered. Anything we need to talk about, or can I have a nap?"

"Rest, Kirby. Dinner at seven in the living room here upstairs?"

"Sure. Sushi."

"Of course. Hugh?"

"Um. Same, I guess?"

"We can order delivery from wherever you want. I'm having Thai, for example."

"Oh. Can I have pizza then? Pepperoni and cheese."

"Great. Kirby, your usual sushi order, and Hugh, pepperoni and cheese for you. I'll see you at seven." With that, he waltzed out.

What now? Kirby stared up at me expectantly. Did he want me to leave or stay? I hadn't seen him since Tuesday. The rain must have enhanced his scent, and the perfume of upcoming heat was slowly filling the room. I pulled it into my lungs, and my dick tingled in my jeans.

"It's raining?"

Kirby wrinkled his nose. "Snowing."

"Already?"

"Yeah."

And nothing.

"I have a room opposite," I said.

"I know."

"But I'll hear the panic button when you press it, so..."

"Yeah."

Fuck, this was awkward. I blew out a breath. "You're tired. I'll leave you be."

Kirby gave me a vague smile. "Thanks."

I waited for him to say something else, but he just looked at me, his expression blank.

"Okay, then."

"See you," he said and began shrugging out of his coat.

I backed out of the room. My entire being ached with the need to be with Kirby. Guess I had to wait for the heat to begin.

As I stood staring at the closed door, I heard Brian's voice coming from one of the rooms down the hall. His tone was unexpectedly harsh. It seemed the gentle, sleek man had a mean streak after all.

"If you ever flip out like this during Kirby's heat, you're out. And this time, I mean it."

Uh-oh. I hid in the other bedroom, popped in my earphones, and put on a podcast.

In the evening, we met all the other staff and crew members. Technicians, assistants, security guys, even cleaning crew. I hadn't had any idea that porn films could have such budgets, but heat porn seemed different, especially on this level. Famous porn stars did only a few of those during their career, so they were considered exclusive. And Kirby was *the* omega of the porn industry. The special edition director's cut would be distributed with a gift box with signed merch and sex toys, and the preorders were already sold out before we'd even started filming. So yes, we had cleaning staff, security, food deliveries, and a stocked bar.

After dinner, the house emptied out. Aside from security, only Brian and Cameron were staying overnight in the downstairs bedrooms just in case Kirby's heat came early. Kirby claimed tiredness again, which was believable with the upcoming heat and all, and closed himself up in the master.

Of course, I couldn't sleep. Instead of tired, I was jittery. In an attempt to exhaust myself, I did push-ups, squats, planks, and crunches, three sets of each, and then two more. I showered. Stretched. Listened to another podcast.

By half past eleven, I was coming out of my skin.

In the hallway, I could just catch the faint scent of Kirby. I paused by the door to the master bedroom and waited if I heard any sound. Nothing.

Hopefully, Kirby was deeply asleep.

I walked to the large living room with floor-to-ceiling windows. Brian must have been loaded as hell to own a house like this. The view would be spectacular during the day. Now, the only thing I could see from the ocean were small blurry lights in the distance where the cargo ships passed on their way to the Dalton City harbor. The wind and waves hummed in the near blackness outside.

I poured myself a glass of water at the bar and walked to the other side of the room. A light sprinkle of snow covered the grounds. The illuminated parking lot and driveway were deserted, but on the lawn in front of the house, right under a lamp, strolled a lone roe deer. It paused, looked around, and hopped off into the darkness.

A quiet padding of bare feet made me turn around. Kirby stood in the middle of the room, wearing sweats and a loose T-shirt. His hair was all over the place and his eyes swollen with sleep.

"Overdid it with the naps. My brain thinks it's morning."

"Hi. I can't fall asleep." I shrugged, and Kirby smirked.

"We're having a good start, then."

"Yeah. Seems so. How are you feeling otherwise?"

"I don't know. Like I'm about to go into heat?"

I smiled. "Meaning?"

"Sleepy, achy, slick all the time." He shrugged. Just as he said it, the scent drifted to me, and I sucked in a breath. Yes, he was close. *Fuck.* He must have been wet because the perfume coming from him immediately brought me back to Tuesday. I could practically taste him. Saliva flooded my mouth at the memory of Kirby coming on my tongue.

He cleared his throat. "I'm sorry I've been avoiding you again."

"I think I get it."

"You do?"

"It's weird. I don't know how to act either."

"Can we talk for a bit? Since we're not sleeping anyway."

"Sure. Something specific you have in mind or just...talk?"

"Both, I guess?"

"Okay."

I sat on the wide sectional, and Kirby joined me, settling next to me.

"I talked to Walter again after Tuesday."

"You did? Why? Did I do something wrong?"

Kirby gave out a half-laugh. "No. You were great."

"Then—"

"The sensations and the orgasms, um, it all got a bit extreme for me."

"I'm sorry, I had no idea. You seemed to like it, and I..."

"I loved it, so chill. Thing is, Walter thinks the heat might get even stronger than last time. Says it happens that heat cycles vary in strength, and since I was this sensitive already before the heat, it might be a sign that we're up against a real scorcher."

"I read up on it and watched all the videos he sent me. I know what to do. I won't leave you hanging, Kirby."

"I know. Thanks."

"But you're worried?"

"I have control issues."

"You're worried about not being in control?"

"I think so."

It was at the tip of my tongue to tell him he should trust me, but that was nonsense. Trust was earned and shouldn't be given blindly.

"It happened briefly with my last heat," Kirby said, "but that wasn't the same."

"How?"

"The wave was peaking, and I had a long breeding orgasm. I couldn't move or do anything, but my head was still clear, you know?"

"And on Tuesday it wasn't?"

He looked away and scratched his neck. He didn't answer.

"Kirby, do you want me to do something? Can I help you feel safer somehow?"

"It's all in my head." He smacked his palm against his forehead, seeming frustrated. "I should be happy because this is like the first heat I'll spend with someone I actually like." He glanced at me, giving me a sad smile that stabbed me into my chest.

I couldn't even imagine what he'd been through before I met him.

"Do you want to talk about it?" I didn't want to hear it, but if he needed to get it out, then I'd sit here, swallow my anger and sadness, and be the most patient listener who'd ever listened.

"No idea. Maybe."

"How was your first heat?" *I don't want to know, dammit.*

Kirby leaned back with his head against the sofa cushion and looked at the ceiling.

"I was nineteen. Been on the street or squatting for three years by then. My shithead of a boyfriend was a dealer. Of course, being an idiot, I thought I loved him. We had a plan. I'd sell the heat to one of his drug bosses who had the hots for me, and we'd take the money and move down south. Except when I was recovering, he bailed. Took the money and vanished. I was such a fool.

Just a kid, you know? But even then, I should have known better."

My stomach tightened, and bile rose into my throat. "That was your first heat?"

"The boss was nice to me. He was forty and experienced. Fucked okay-ish, fed me, let me stay for a couple of days after so I could get through the worst of the recovery. And he paid what he'd promised. He told me to take the money myself and go, but like I said, I was dumb."

"And then?"

"Then I began selling ass."

Glistening eyes aimed upward, he made a scoffing sound and folded his arms over his chest.

"Learned quickly what was safe and who to avoid. But it was a dark time for me. I don't think about those months anymore. Then I found Emerson, a fourteen-year-old kid, freezing and hungry, and life got bearable again."

"You took care of him for years."

"He was like a baby bird, so scared. He trusted me from day one, like he imprinted on me or something. I felt better about myself thanks to him. Yeah, I was a rent boy and occasionally stole shit at supermarkets, but I kept Emerson out of trouble. The little fucker wanted to help earn money." Kirby made quotation marks with his fingers saying the word 'help,' and I got what he meant. He glanced at me meaningfully. "Burke knows, by the way, and doesn't give a damn."

"He loves Emerson."

"Yeah, he does. It's nice to see. Anyway. Emerson soon realized that sucking dick for cash wasn't as glamorous as it was made out to be and stopped. He kept looking for work but always ended up screwed over in one way or another. I tried to get a good deal for my second heat so we could rent a room somewhere for the winter, and I thought I'd managed. The guy was a mean asshole who liked to tie me up for the heat waves, but he had a nice place, and it wasn't a chore staying there. Except when it was all done, he gave me barely half of what he'd promised. Threatened to call the police on me and say I'd robbed him if I kept arguing, so I left. We spent the winter in and out of shelters."

Okay. This was like being raked over hot coals. I gripped his hand. I just needed to touch him, hold him, and thank heavens, he let me.

"Then I had a good guy lined up for my third, but he cancelled on me last minute because he met someone he wanted to date for real. Desperate, I let a couple of regulars share me. They bought me the contraceptive pills, but treated me like shit and kicked me out hours after the last heatwave without pay. I got a nasty infection after that one. I think that was the only time Emerson stole something. I was trying to wash myself in the park bathrooms, and he came with an antibiotic cream. Must have been expensive as fuck, and there was no way he had the cash. But it literally saved my ass." He chuckled humorlessly.

"So you see, the heat movie I did with Brian was basically paradise. Four alphas, professionals with an impeccable reputation. Walter Sébastien sat there like the heat police, and Brian went on and on about omega pleasure. And the guys treated me like I was royalty on and off camera. But first and foremost, it was *safe*. I loved it." He smirked. "As was obvious. I mean, you saw the peaking heat wave in the middle. I was basically delirious."

"I haven't seen it," I croaked.

Kirby lifted his head and looked at me with a confused frown. "You haven't seen it?"

"No. I...haven't seen any of your films."

That made him sit up straight. "What?"

"It felt private."

"Private? It's porn, Hugh. Everybody and their dads have seen me fuck. Why?" He seemed torn between laughter and outrage.

"You're a friend. It felt wrong. Like spying on you or something. And then you got more and more famous, and it became this huge thing... I couldn't."

Kirby just stared at me, stunned. "Wow. What the hell are you even doing here?"

Then he spurred into action. He pulled his phone out of the pocket of his sweats and began typing.

"Look."

Kirby Matthews breeding scene

Oh shit.

He clicked on the third hit and shoved the phone in front of my nose.

"Gotta pop that cherry, Hughie," he said and tapped on the play icon.

My neck grew hot and my groin tight.

Kirby was sitting in a guy's lap, his back to the alpha's chest. He was bouncing up and down in the alpha's embrace who thrust into him from below, shoving his long dick in and out of Kirby's hole. Two other alphas lay by Kirby's sides, sucking on his nipples vigorously and rubbing their exposed knots on Kirby's body where they could reach. A fourth man stood above Kirby, his cock also swollen with a painful looking, throbbing knot at the underside. Kirby suckled on it mindlessly, his face and chest covered with pearls of cum.

Then the camera zeroed in on Kirby's middle. His balls tight, his cock dancing, spitting small drops of seed, his hole clenching endlessly. An echoing roar came from the speakers, and Kirby's belly seemed to bulge. He shivered and twitched, and his hole let out an excess of wetness over the alpha's balls.

"The guys made my nipples come while Dex bred me. I left my body at that moment."

Kirby's voice seemed to be coming from afar. Blood pulsed in my ears, and my cock throbbed in my pants.

Kirby closed the app and put the phone on the coffee table.

I barely knew where I was.

"So. Now you know."

"I..." I cleared my throat. "I get it now. Why the film is so famous."

Kirby grinned. "Hot, huh? Look at that tent." He pointed at my groin and bit his lip.

"Fuck's sake, Kirby."

I bent over and held my head in my hands, trying to get a grip. Inhale, exhale, inhale, exhale.

I'll get to fuck him soon. Knot him.

Except I only had to remember those stories, those men who'd used him in the past, to get my libido under control.

He's never had a heat with someone he liked.

"Sorry, Hugh," Kirby piped up next to me. "I wanted to lighten up the mood."

Taking another deep breath, I turned to him on the sofa.

"Thank you for telling me all of that. Before you showed the clip."

"You're thanking me? You looked like you were about to puke."

"Did you ever talk about it with someone else?"

"Yeah. Walter cleaned up my head before the filming two years ago. He's good."

"He is. And what you said before, about your fear of losing control, is it because of what happened to you?"

"Maybe. But I'm not afraid that you would treat me badly."

"What are you afraid of, then?"

"It's hard to describe. Like I'm afraid to just...let myself enjoy it."

The need to hold him grew even stronger. I threw my arm over him, hoping he wouldn't move away. Kirby lay his head on my chest, and I hugged him to me, grateful.

"But I trust you, Hugh," he said quietly.

I exhaled with relief. We sat in silence while I slowly sorted through the mess in my head: Kirby's horrendous sexual history, the trauma he must carry, consciously or subconsciously, the breezy way he talked about some things...and then the sight of him in the throes of a breeding orgasm, surrounded by alphas who seemed to worship him like a god.

After all of that, here I was. Just little old me.

How the hell was I supposed to make it good for him? With a film crew on my ass?

He snuggled in my arms, humming quietly, and I stroked his back up and down through the thin T-shirt. A blanket lay folded over the armrest, so I grabbed it and threw it over Kirby.

"Thanks. But I'm going to go to bed."

"Stay for just one more minute."

"Just a minute," he agreed.

Except he fell asleep.

I breathed in his scent before I nodded off myself.

When I woke up to gray skies outside, I was alone and

had a crick in my neck. The blanket was spread out over me.

I stood and walked over to the ocean view, stretching my back. A small figure dressed in black wandered along the waves outside. I wanted to go and join him, but I wouldn't. Apparently, Kirby had wanted a break, and an early-morning, lonesome walk on a beach might be just what he needed.

He acted unaffected, telling me about his life like it was nothing, but what he must have been through... Fuck. I didn't know what to do with all the anger.

Watching him wander on the beach, I could see only one solution. I'd channel all my frustration into giving him pleasure. I'd make this the best heat any omega had ever had.

I'd treat him like a fucking prince. Or...I could do even better.

I'd treat him like the love of my life.

CHAPTER 10

KIRBY

Barely awake, I smacked the panic button with the back of my hand. After my last heat at the studio, it must have become a reflex—the first sign of a wave, just a twinge in my lower back, and I was reaching for the button.

Brian burst into the room in his pajamas with Hugh on his heels.

"Are you okay?" Hugh blurted.

"Calm down," I grumbled. "We've got time."

I sat up on the bed, and he hovered awkwardly. "Can I get you anything?"

"Water?"

I handed him the empty glass from the nightstand, and he took it, presumably heading to the bar in the living room.

"How are you feeling, Kirby?"

"We got a few minutes before it's full on."

"Good. I want some foreplay. We're only waiting for Cameron."

131

Right then, the cameraman came in, buttoning up his jeans.

"Hi. Show time?"

"Yes." Brian rubbed his hands, like always.

Hugh brought two tall glasses with water and two extra bottles plus straws.

"Put the bottles under the bed, Hugh," Brian said. "We can't have any labels in the frame."

"Oh. Sure."

"Cameron?"

He was tightening a support vest with a stabilizer around his torso. Since he was relatively slight, he used the mechanical arm to hold the heavy camera at odd angles. "Cameras one and two are running. Thirty seconds and I'm good to go with number three." Brian walked over to the stationary cameras and glanced at the screens. "The lighting has been ready since yesterday."

A sudden flood of light blinded me before my eyes slowly adjusted.

"Great," Brian said. "Guys. The first three waves, I'll give you more specific instructions, and once we have that, we can freestyle the rest. Now I want kissing on the bed and teasing. As long as we have time for. Kirby, when you feel it getting stronger, show me all the needy, no holding back on me. Feel free to move around, but the knotting should happen while Hugh spoons you on the bed with your legs spread, so we can get a close-up."

I glanced at Hugh, who was glaring at Brian with an expression that could be translated as focus—if you didn't know him. He was annoyed. I wouldn't say I told him so, but I'd told him so.

"We're good to go," Cameron said.

Brian clapped, and it was quiet.

Hugh just stood there, unmoving, looking at me. He seemed a little stunned.

So I raised my eyebrows at him and pulled the duvet off me. I was naked underneath.

That made him move.

He climbed onto the bed and leaned close, his eyes searching mine. Like he was asking for permission again. His scent reached my nose, musky and woodsy, and my insides quivered. The buildup might be shorter than Brian thought.

I lifted my hand and gently placed it on the side of Hugh's neck.

"This is it," I whispered. "Ready?"

Instead of replying, he dove in.

In the tangle of emotions, the one I could recognize was relief. Maybe. As soon as our tongues touched, all the tension I'd carried for the past few days seemed to melt away. Had I missed him? He tasted like home. I dismissed the idea as soon as it occurred to me. As if I knew what home was... Wrapping his strong arms around me, he lay on top of me, and my legs opened for him automatically. His erection pressed against mine.

I whimpered when I felt a ghost of a cramp in my middle. No, we didn't have nearly as much time as I'd thought.

"We need to hurry," I mumbled against his lips.

Swiftly, Hugh rolled us and tugged me up until I straddled his chest. Then he gripped my ass cheeks and sucked my cock into his mouth.

I gasped.

"Excellent," Brian enthused, and I wished he'd shut up for the rest of the fucking week.

Hugh sucked me to the hilt and pulled my ass cheeks

apart, exposing my crease. The wetness I was leaking dribbled down my taint and my balls. I clenched and unclenched a few times, the emptiness getting worse. But Hugh must have known because he pushed two fingers into me. The sudden fullness helped, and I rocked my hips, fucking into his mouth.

My pleasure built fast, and when he added a third finger from his other hand, pulling my hole open, I came. The climax washed over me, making me cry out and shudder. Intense but unsatisfying. A hot ball of energy in my core grew and grew, pulsating, and I whined, my hips jerking.

"Your ass fucking squirted, Kirby. Gorgeous. You're doing great."

Shut the fuck up!

"Please, Hugh," I whispered. "Please."

Hugh grabbed me by my waist and threw me sideways. He lifted my legs, folded me in half, and looked at my hole. Cameron was right there next to him, but I did my best to delete him from my mind. Just Hugh and me.

The crew used to be a comforting thing while I was getting plowed on set. My safety net. But when Hugh touched me, they were noise.

Running his thumb over my opening, Hugh hummed, smearing my slick around. He licked the pad of his finger and gripped the base of his cock. Then the bastard tapped his erection over my open, aching hole.

I wailed.

The emptiness got painful, and a harsh cramp squeezed my middle.

"Need my knot?"

"Please."

Placing his big hands on the back of my thighs, he

pressed me into the mattress. The position squeezed my stomach, making the cramps bearable for a moment.

"Mewling little kitten."

"Give me your cock, please. Please, Hugh."

"Shh, I got you."

The pressure caught me off guard at first, but then I remembered. Hugh was *thick*. My body opened eagerly, welcoming him in, and I gave out a long groan of sheer gratitude.

Like flipping a switch. Nothing mattered but that cock. The scent. The warmth of the man all over me.

Holding me tight, Hugh pumped into me with slow, steady strokes, to the root on each thrust, and my cum trickled out of my slit and onto my belly as my orgasm rose higher.

I was mewling, all right.

Such a good cock.

Heat was always way different than a regular fuck. Nerve endings came alive I didn't know I had. The tissue in my hole got super soft, and my gland swelled, the bump extra sensitive. The mouth to my womb sank low and got hungry, so every brush of a cockhead over it sent both yearning and delight through me. The orgasms were something else. I came more often, sometimes for minutes on end, and the pleasure rose and fell in waves. But they weren't satisfactory like a normal climax. Nope. They were sharp-edged and mean. Every peak only wound me up and left me craving more. Aside from all of that, my nipples got tight and tingly, my erection throbbed, and my balls drew up. Climax after climax, my insides loosened until I felt like one big, cavernous hole, achingly hungry, coming endlessly but never satiated. And that's when I needed a knot to make it all stop.

Hugh's thrusts gathered strength, and he moved like a machine, in and out, harder, and harder still. I was so full of slick my ass squelched, liquid bubbling up. He changed angle, fucking me a little to the side, and the wrongness of it had me squirming. To the other side. Downward. Oh my God, up! Fuck yeah! Right over my gland and close to the mouth to my womb. I keened with another powerful peak.

And then he pulled out.

I wailed, bucking, but Hugh was there. He spooned me and shoved his perfect cock back into me. Holding my right leg by my thigh, he held me spread open and fucked me hard, our skin slapping together.

He grazed his teeth over my neck, and I bent my head, giving him access. I wanted him to bite me.

"Hugh."

"What, little kitten?"

"Knot me. Please."

"Shh. Not yet." Hugh, the bastard, had taken my bold talk at Walter's office too seriously.

I bowed, pushing my ass into his lap, and he gripped me tighter. With his other hand, he covered my throat and caught my jaw. He forcibly pulled my face to him and kissed me.

I hadn't known I needed that. His tongue in my mouth soothed me, and I hummed, suckling on it.

His hardness pumped in and out of me, my hole gradually wetter and looser, until there was no resistance at all. I felt like jelly. Like I was melting away and Hugh's cock was my only connection to life. Blindly, I grappled at his thigh. He wouldn't pull out anymore, would he? He wouldn't leave me hanging. He broke the kiss, and I forced my eyes open. I found his gaze pinned on me, black and dangerous. Possessive. He was gorgeous.

"Please," I breathed against his lips. I couldn't find my voice. "Please."

"You really need it now, don't you?"

I nodded vigorously, letting out a pathetic whimper.

Hugh licked into my mouth again. His thrusts got vicious, all but punching the sealed gate to my core, and my lower body exploded with another wave of pleasure. Growling against my lips, Hugh nestled himself deep inside me, holding me in place by my hip. His cock jerked.

My eyes rolled into the back of my head. There it was. The stretch. The delicious, amazing stretch. The knot grew, pulsating with Hugh's release, pushing on my gland while Hugh's cum filled me. This was the climax I'd been waiting for. Profound and powerful, like a fucking reboot of my entire nervous system, turning my brain into a mashed sweet potato.

Except the knot kept growing.

I twitched involuntarily, the pressure on my gland too much. Hugh smoothed his hand over my underbelly.

"Shh, kitty. You can take it. You were made for this."

He squeezed my cock and stroked it, and the tension dissipated. His erection kept jerking inside me, the knot getting even bigger. I gasped, but this time, it was with pleasure.

Fucking hell, he was huge.

He pushed his thumb between my lips and kept milking my shaft. I sucked on instinct, tasting my own slick and cum, and Hugh rocked us, gently thrusting.

Biggest fucking knot ever. Did my hips widen? And when it moved in me, pushing and pulling on my insides, tingles exploded from my gland, spreading all over my body.

Impossibly, I came once more. The king of all orgasms

made me arch and shake, my mewls muted with Hugh's thumb in my mouth. I sucked on it vigorously, trying to remain sane as fire and ice chased each other through my veins.

He snapped his hips forward, shoving the giant knot even deeper, and I might have left my body for a second. The keening cry I made must have rattled the windows.

Fuck, I was so full. So fucking full. The climax slowly simmered, like electric currents running up and down my spread, limp legs. I would never be able to close them again.

Not that I wanted to.

The enormous swollen cock lodged in me was the most precious gift on earth.

I panted, shivering. Was it over? Was I still coming? It felt so fucking good. How come it didn't hurt? I'd never had anything so huge in me. My inner muscles slowly adjusted until I felt like I was made of cooked noodles.

Taking deep breaths, I relaxed into the feeling, letting it flow through me. Like sinking into a hot tub.

Hugh covered my twitching cock and balls with his warm palm, kneading softly.

"It's okay, love. It's done now. You've done so well. It's all inside you now. Such a good, big hole. I told you I'd fill you up. You're so sweet, my little kitten. Will you purr for me? Are you happy?"

He kept rocking us, subtly moving inside me and stroking my tongue with his thumb. I did purr.

I'd never been happier.

CHAPTER 11

HUGH

Kirby was barely conscious. I'd never seen anyone come as hard as he did when I fucked him with my knot. He'd looked ecstatic.

The dangerous sense of ownership was back in full force. I held him to me by his cum-drenched groin, gagging him with my thumb, and I fucked him gently with the knot, savoring his helpless shivers. He made sounds of pure delight, like I was feeding him something delicious. Ever so slowly, as he quieted, I stopped moving and pulled my thumb out of his mouth.

I kissed the side of his face, ignoring Cameron who hovered right above us with his stupid robot arm and a cannon of an objective. Closing my eyes, I breathed Kirby in and brushed his skin with my lips. He nuzzled back, and his hand found mine over his groin. Interlacing our fingers, he got heavier in my embrace.

My knot tingled inside him, and his hole squeezed me from time to time in an aftershock. I lifted my head and brushed his lips with mine. He opened up with a sigh, giving me his tongue to lick and suck on. The lazy kiss went on and on.

My knot was no way near shrinking, and as Kirby kissed me back, my cock let out a few more drops of cum. He wiggled a little, as if testing our joining, and it made us both groan.

I briefly thought of Walter's four words. Aggressive, possessive, caring, and protective. Had I been aggressive with Kirby? A little maybe? But fuck, the possessiveness flared up, burning through me.

"Cameron. We're good for now. Let them rest. We'll do the aftercare when Trent's here."

Thank you, Brian.

"Guys, all three cameras are off now," Brian said.

Neither of us replied.

Soon, the shuffling quieted, and the door closed. Peering at the room around us, I realized with relief we were alone.

"Hey, kitten, you okay?"

"Uh-huh." He squeezed my hand and gave me a small peck on the lips.

"Was it good for you?"

"You weren't kidding about the size of your knot."

"I know. I tried to warn you."

"It feels amazing. It made me come so hard."

"Good. Are you comfortable?"

"A little cold."

I grabbed the duvet that was bunched up next to me and dragged it over us. Kirby sighed.

"Thanks."

"You can sleep if you want."

"No need. I'm hungry, though. Once the knot goes down, I need to eat something. What time is it anyway?"

"It was five in the morning when you hit the panic button. So maybe around six?"

"That's ridiculously early."

I couldn't stop kissing and caressing him. I peppered his cheek and temple with small pecks, and he smiled softly.

"This is nice. I'm all mellow. I'm not usually like this."

"How are you usually?"

"Waiting for the knot to deflate is the awkward part unless I'm tired enough to fall asleep."

"And it's not awkward now?"

He kissed my nose. "No. It's delicious. At some point, I want to see it."

"My knot?"

"Uh-huh."

"I've heard it hurts if it grows outside."

"Not if I take care of it." He winked, the tip of his tongue peeking out between his lips. His playful smirk and dancing eyes made happiness surge in my chest.

My omega. For how long? But I wouldn't think about that. I had ten days. Ten whole days of fucking him, taking care of him, and maybe even showing him how it felt to be loved.

"Can I stay here, Kirby?"

"Not like you can go anywhere now."

"I mean sleep here. With you."

His expression turned thoughtful. "I'm not used to sleeping with anyone."

"I don't want to be away from you. Walter said that I might get protective and...demanding, remember?" In reality, the thought of being away from him made me want to

141

handcuff him to me and throw away the keys. The pheromones were already affecting me.

"I don't mind. Like I said, I like this." He wiggled again, and I tightened my arms around him.

I felt the pressure in my knot relent a little. It would soon go down.

Kirby sighed from deep within when I pulled my softening cock out.

"Shower?" I asked and offered him my hand.

"Sure."

He let me hold his hand and set the water temperature for him, and then he let me wash his back and ass. I soaped up his soft cock and balls, and he leaned into my arms, humming.

"I could get used to this."

"Pampering? Feel free. I love doing it. Besides, you're sexy all wet and slippery."

"Turn around. I'll do your back."

Kirby's long-fingered hands massaged my shoulders and down along my spine, and I closed my eyes under the spray of hot water.

"Kirby, um, we should keep talking, right? Was it all good for you? Is there something you'd like me to do differently next time?"

"I think we went faster than Brian wanted us to, but honestly, I needed it. The heat wave came with a vengeance, and considering it was the first, I don't know how much time we'll have for foreplay and showing off. I think we might have to do some faking after all and film extra stuff between waves."

"Kirby, I didn't mean the filming. I meant you and me."

He paused for a second, and then his hands slid to my butt, kneading. I widened my stance, and he ran his fingers through my crease, making me shiver. He cupped my balls and squeezed gently.

"You're amazing, Hugh. I have zero complaints."

He stepped closer and plastered his front to my back, running his hands down my stomach to my half-hard cock. He weighed it in his hands.

"You'll make me change my mind about sleeping with friends. I love having sex with you." *Friends.* Well, fuck. "I was so nervous about it, but now, I feel great. Thank you for that."

"I really want to make it good for you, Kirby." *Nobody will ever use you or hurt you again. I'll make sure of it.*

"You're doing a great job so far." He squeezed my shaft and let go. With a pat over my butt, he stepped out of the shower and reached for a bathrobe. "Breakfast?"

"Yes please."

CHAPTER 12

KIRBY

I had never been able to come between heat waves, and the idea of sex didn't really appeal at the moment. But like I'd told Hugh, Brian did think we'd rushed it last time and wanted some slow, lazy lurve.

Cameron double-checked the lighting was the same and left Trent in charge before going home for the day.

Hugh lay on top of me as he'd done in the morning, and Brian fumbled with the sheets and duvet, bringing them into roughly the same disorder they'd been at the beginning of the first wave. Even the glasses of water were in place. He compared the result with the footage he'd saved on his tablet and nodded to himself.

A perfect fake like always.

"Action."

That stupid word. Sounded so pretentious somehow.

Braced on his arms, Hugh hovered above me, his eyes roaming my face. He must have read my irritation because he smiled sadly at me. "Close your eyes, kitten. I'll make it good. Promise."

He really was too good for this world, wasn't he?

"It's okay. Let's work."

He shook his head and leaned in close to my ear. "No. Don't think about work. Just close your eyes."

His lips brushed the hollow in front of my ear and down under my jaw. Hot wet tongue, a nip. Slow nuzzle. He kissed and nipped his way to my nipple and gently suckled on it. I prepared myself for the bite, the prospect unappealing now that I wasn't aroused, but he didn't use his teeth at all. He only kissed and licked gently before continuing down my torso to my belly button. He mapped my chest and stomach with kisses, caressing my sides and ribs with his broad, calloused hands.

Whenever I thought he was done, he started all over again. My collarbones, slow wet kisses down the center of my chest, over my hipbones... Until I didn't have to focus on keeping my eyes shut and staying still. I just lay there, his for the moment, my legs and arms heavy, muscles relaxed.

After slowly turning me around, he climbed up the bed until he covered my body. He was hard against my crease, and he thrust teasingly, dragging his thick cock between my ass cheeks. Brian would like that.

But I didn't have to think about Brian. Hugh would take care of everything.

He nipped at my neck and kneaded the muscles in my upper back before kissing down my spine. Wet, open-mouthed kisses covered my lower back and the dimples above my ass. I felt myself relax deeper into the mattress.

When Hugh kissed the top of my crease and licked the spot, I parted my legs for him. I trusted him. Implicitly.

Between waves, any penetration would be painful, but he knew. He nuzzled my crease, kissed the insides of my thighs, and gently opened me up. The hot, wet tongue on my oversensitive rim was a surprising delight.

I'd never been rimmed between waves either.

Why was it weird?

It felt amazing. Gentle and caring, the sensations delicious. What was nagging at me?

The crew? No. I could easily pretend they didn't exist. I could only smell and feel Hugh.

Why was it strange?

He dragged his tongue over my loose rim and kissed the tender, heated skin. Nobody had ever been so careful with me. Caring. Selfless.

Thing was, I knew Hugh wasn't doing it for the cameras. He did it for me. That was the weird thing rattling around in my confused brain. Hugh was the first lover I'd ever had who did something *just for me*. The thought almost brought tears to my eyes, but then his tongue delved inside, just the tip, and I groaned from deep in my belly.

Impossibly, I got hard.

Hugh rolled me again and sucked my shaft to the hilt. He alternated between rimming me and licking my cock, and soon I was writhing. Could I come between waves after all? It was only the beginning of the heat. Maybe? Hugh's wriggling tongue delved deeper, and I moaned. Yeah. Yeah, I'd come.

"I'm close," I whispered, and Hugh grinned up at me before sucking me to the root again. He went back to my hole but wrapped his hand around my shaft. Desperate, I gripped the covers. The relief was unbelievable. A slow, lazy climax spilled from my hole into my belly and down my thighs, followed by comforting warmth.

Hugh sucked the slick out of me and licked the few drops of my cum. Then he crawled up my body and wrapped his arms around me. I kissed him and stroked his cock.

"You can touch me, kitten, but don't make me come, okay?"

It felt hot against my palm, velvet over steel, and I could barely wrap my fingers around it.

Trent hovered above us, focused on Hugh's magnificent dick, but I only looked at Hugh. His eyes were warm, content, maybe even a little smug.

"This was perfect, guys. We got what I wanted. Let's take a break until the next wave."

No.

I wasn't done exploring.

Hugh, thank hell, dragged the duvet over us and didn't let go of me. I hid my face in his chest and waited until the crew left, closing the door behind them. Then I wrapped my hand around Hugh's cock again.

"I meant it," he rasped. "I don't want to come now. I need to wait for the next wave."

"I know. But I want to play with your dick."

He groaned, sounding a little frustrated. "Sure. Whatever."

"It's so warm and heavy."

"You're killing me, Kirby."

"You're the first guy who ever made me come between waves. It was interesting."

"It sounded like a good one."

"Sweet, mild, and very satisfying."

"Good."

I squeezed the base of his cock and nipped at his lips. He grinned and kissed me. Lightly stroking along his length, I caressed his tongue with mine. Such a lovely cock. I really truly didn't want to let go of it.

Except Hugh grabbed my wrist and pinned my hand by my shoulder. His smile looked slightly predatory.

"That's enough for now," he said sternly, and I pouted.

"It's mine for the heat."

"Greedy kitty." He bit my lower lip.

Then he pushed off the bed and strode to the bathroom.

"You'll get it back in a few hours, don't worry," he threw over his shoulder and closed himself in there. Soon, the sound of the shower came through the door.

I sprawled on the bed, frowning at the ceiling.

I felt good. I felt so damn good with Hugh.

Which made me apprehensive as fuck.

CHAPTER 13

HUGH

With the third wave, I had a system. Flawless compartmentalization. The crew was somewhere in the periphery, and a part of my brain seemed to be low-key aware of them. My body made the correct moves to let the cameras in on the action without me needing to focus on it. The flow of time was another compartment—necessary to be conscious of it, but again, not the focus. All of that happened in the background while my entire being zeroed in on Kirby. His breaths, scent, his languid movements and sighs of pleasure, his blown pupils, the traces his nails made on my back and ass cheeks, the taste of his kisses on my tongue... My beautiful, horny omega.

His hand was on my cock again. He seemed to like touching it, always reaching for it even between waves, as if it was a comfort thing for him. Now as his need built, he stroked the length and whined from the back of his throat. Then he swiftly rolled onto his knees and grabbed the headboard. He pushed his ass out, curving his spine, and stared at me with big, needy eyes.

He moaned when I slowly got onto my knees and took my time getting into position. I ran my fingers through his drenched crease. His hole was puffy and pink, swollen with heat, and it dilated right in front of my eyes, letting out another trickle of syrupy slick. Kirby whimpered. He must have been getting uncomfortable.

The tip of my cock kissed his rim, and Kirby rattled the headboard, his knuckles white. My poor little kitten.

With a steady, firm thrust, I filled him to the hilt. His slick, hot flesh cushioned my erection, then tightened around it, and he cried out with what sounded like raw joy.

A mere five thrusts, and he came.

Oh, I loved this. I adored giving him pleasure, and it was so damn easy. Wherever I touched him, he soaked it up like a damned sponge. I had never accomplished anything as gratifying as making Kirby come.

I hauled him up to improve the angle for him, and he gripped my forearm with both hands, holding on for dear life. With a few measured thrusts, I fucked another climax out of him. His bouncing erection sprayed heat cum all over the pillows. I didn't want the crew to change the bedding this time. I'd love to sleep on those and breathe in the scent of Kirby's pleasure all night long.

The juices he leaked wetted my thighs, and his hole milked my cock with powerful spasms. Roping both arms around him, I squeezed him to me when the knot grew. Kirby keened, shivering like a leaf.

The hold of his inner muscles around my pulsing knot was absolutely delicious. Maybe I imagined it, but I thought I felt the mouth to his womb right there, against my cockhead, kissing my throbbing cock and soaking up my cum. I pushed a little deeper, and yeah, there it was. The gate to paradise. I'd fuck it open soon. Kirby would need it.

The thought of breeding him made my cock jerk again with another wave of release. Kirby panted, his legs shaking, so I turned onto my back, bringing him with me. He slumped in my lap, his back to my chest, and I rocked his limp body on my knot.

His guttural moans let me know how much he loved it. He anchored himself with his hands on the back of my neck and bore down onto my swollen cock. I gripped his hips to hold him in place.

"Can I keep going?" I whispered into his ear. "Want to fuck you with my knot."

"Uh-huh. Please. So good. Love your cock. Your knot. So fucking big."

"Hold on, kitten."

I braced my feet on the mattress and tilted my hips, thrusting upward. Kirby let out a loud cry of what sounded like ecstasy. The alpha in me beat his chest.

I didn't know how many times I'd made him come. It sounded like one long continuous climax. By the time I spurted another load of cum into his open body, he was a sobbing mess.

Hugging him to me, I curled up around him, spooning him on the bed. His limp body twitched from time to time, so I cradled his still-hard cock in my hand and massaged it. It seemed to soothe him, and soon his breathing evened out.

He fell asleep.

I lifted myself on my arm, supporting my head in my hand, and gazed at his profile. He was so beautiful in his sleep. Vulnerable and trusting.

The cameras and lights hummed like a swarm of bees, the sound getting louder in my head. I wanted to cover Kirby up so the other people in the room couldn't get to him. So they couldn't use him.

Trent knelt on the bed with us, getting close-ups of Kirby's swollen belly and my hand on his softening cock, and I wanted to hurl slurs at the poor guy. He was stealing this perfect moment from me.

So much for my perfect compartmentalization.

I exchanged a look with Brian, and understanding seemed to flash in the director's eyes.

"Trent. We're good," he said.

I mouthed a thank you, and he gave me a small smile.

Within minutes, Kirby and I were alone, the room illuminated only by a single lamp on the nightstand.

I held my Kirby as he slept, nuzzling his hair, unable to fall asleep myself. My knot receded, but I didn't pull out. Kirby seemed comfortable, and I didn't want to wake him up. Or no, that was just an excuse. I simply wanted to stay inside him for as long as he'd let me. Every once in a while, a reminder popped up in my head, unwelcome and jarring, that my little slice of heaven had an expiration date.

I MUST HAVE FINALLY DOZED off myself because next, I woke to the scent of fresh coffee.

Kirby sat on the bed in his bathrobe, his hair wet from the shower. He handed me a mug, so I scrambled up and leaned against the headboard.

"Thank you." I took a grateful sip. "What time is it?"

"Ten in the morning."

"Fuck. We slept for what, nine hours?"

"Maybe even longer. I don't remember when I fell asleep last night."

"You were still knotted."

"Mmm. Yeah. That was great, by the way. Thank you."

"Happy to be of service." I winked, and Kirby smirked into his coffee mug. "They kept shooting after you fell asleep, so Brian has some footage of you out of it."

"Okay," he said breezily.

He'd been filmed in so many vulnerable situations, no privacy left, and he didn't seem bothered by it. And I'd be a hypocrite to think he should be bothered since I sometimes experienced wild surges of arousal knowing others would see me fucking and *owning* Kirby. So why did it bug me they kept filming after he'd fallen asleep?

I couldn't protect him.

Stupid, irrational alpha urges. Stupid pheromones.

Kirby unwrapped a protein bar and handed me another. "This okay? I'm afraid the next wave could come within an hour or so."

"Sure. Thanks. I better do a quick visit to the bathroom then."

"You do that. I just want to lie down."

He finished his coffee and settled onto the pillows, munching on the bar. I ate mine in four bites and dashed to the bathroom. Being separated from Kirby, even though it was only by a thin bathroom door, made me deeply uneasy.

After brushing my teeth, I took a swift shower. I was back by Kirby's side in a few minutes.

"Are you okay?" he asked.

I startled. "Sure. Why?"

He shrugged, looking uncharacteristically insecure. "You seem annoyed."

Oh. "I'm okay. You don't have to worry about me."

"So you won't hate me for dragging you into this." He looked down at his hands, folding and unfolding the empty protein bar wrapper. His voice had a sharp edge.

I took the wrapper from him and threw it into the basket by the door. Then I climbed onto the bed and pulled him to me. His catlike eyes seemed wary, and I knew that expression very well. His defenses were up.

"Kirby, you didn't drag me into anything. I insisted, remember?"

He lowered his gaze.

"I'm not regretting a single moment," I said, tightening my hold on him. "Fucking you, making love to you, is a damned privilege. And sure, sometimes I wish the crew would go and fuck themselves and film *that* instead. But that has nothing to do with you."

"But it has, don't you get it? This is who I am."

"This is just one of the things that you *do*, Kirby."

"No difference."

I wouldn't go into a discussion about words and their definitions. Kirby could so easily misunderstand. I would never think less of him because he did porn or suggest he quit and pursue a more 'dignified' career. He shouldn't be ashamed of his job. It was my job now as well, right? "Kirby, you are an amazing performer. You should be proud." He frowned before his gaze widened in surprise. "You've made so many people feel empowered. The last heat film you made shifted an entire generation's view on omegas in pornography. You're a living legend, kitten."

He scoffed softly but didn't interrupt me.

"And it makes me so hot thinking that people will watch this movie and envy me. Not because I got to knot *the* Kirby Matthews, even though that's cool as fuck."

Kirby giggled, shaking his head like I was being silly.

"But because they will see how much pleasure we give each other. How much we love touching each other. They'll hear your cries when I knot you and see me tremble with aftershocks, and they'll know that we've fucked each other's brains out. They'll notice how you give yourself to me with absolute trust and let me do whatever I want with you. Every alpha in the fucking world will want to be me." I lowered my voice. "But they can't because you're mine now." *For the duration of the heat* was implied. "I can get annoyed when Cameron hovers above us like a vulture, waiting for his precious cum shot, but that's a small price to pay for everything. Do you believe me?"

"I think I do."

"And you? Are you okay? The loss of control you talked about..."

"Yeah." He smiled gently and gave me a small peck on the lips. "I've been out of control since the first wave, Hugh. But it's okay because you've been taking care of me. I'm not afraid anymore. I trust you."

My heart squeezed at his simple admission. I didn't say anything, worried my voice would betray my emotion. I kissed him instead and hugged him on the bed, dragging the covers over us.

"I'm afraid we'll have to push the panic button soon."

"How soon?"

"I don't know. Anything between five and twenty minutes."

"Can I hold you until we have to do that?"

"Yes."

He sighed and snuggled closer. One-handed, I shot a quick text to Jay, just checking in. Then I put my phone under the bed and roped both arms around Kirby.

CHAPTER 14

KIRBY

I was addicted to his hands. All soaped up, they felt even better. With just the right amount of strength to remind me how dangerous he could be, he squeezed and kneaded my muscles, from my shoulders, over my bloated pecs, to my ass and thighs, until I was barely holding myself upright with my palms braced on the tiles.

After rinsing me, Hugh turned the water off and knelt behind me in the shower stall. He parted my ass cheeks and shoved his tongue into my hole. I was fucked out and stretched after the knotting, my rim loose, the mix of cum and slick dribbling out of me, and he licked into all of that with a possessive growl.

"Show me," Brian said.

Hugh held my crease spread for the camera. My hole must have looked like puckered lips. When I ran my fingers over my rim, I could feel how it stuck out, swollen and raw. Hugh massaged my ass cheeks, and another dollop of bodily fluids leaked out of me.

"Nice," Trent muttered.

Ugh.

The random comments the crew said from time to time didn't use to bother me. But just like Hugh, I was getting annoyed with them.

As if he'd heard my thoughts, Hugh dove into my crease, shielding my most vulnerable part from view. He licked me slowly and tenderly, the swipes of his tongue soothing my oversensitive skin, and I let out a moan.

"Don't stop," I heard myself say.

I felt the arousal budding in my core, a small ball of coiled heat growing bigger ever so slowly. The last heat wave had ended barely an hour ago, but another one was coming already.

Hugh must have smelled and tasted it because he licked into me with force. An ache like nothing I'd ever felt before bloomed in my womb, and I gasped.

All the demons in hell! This was it. Sure, I'd been keen during heat before, but I'd only ever heard about *this* level of horniness. This was the famous omega need that had been driving the population numbers for millennia. *I must get knocked up or die.* Thank fuck for contraceptives because no way in hell would I have made it through this wave without cum up my womb.

"Hugh. Breed me," I begged.

"Need a new battery, Brian," Trent said urgently.

Steps sounded in the bathroom, and the door banged.

"Here."

The sounds registered in some closed-off part of my mind, as if coming from behind a wall. The noises Hugh made, though, were loud and distinct. Sucking, slurping, humming... Fuck, I was so wet. Had I been this wet during my last heat? Maybe after a wave, but this...

Hugh kept tongue-fucking me, and it felt brilliant, until a cramp gripped my underbelly and I yelped.

"Hugh!"

Swiftly, he hoisted me up. He sat me on top of the bathroom counter and lifted my legs. In seconds, his fat cock was stretching my bruised walls anew.

He was relentless. Harsh, powerful thrusts, his cockhead hitting the mouth to my womb on each fuck. I was so overstimulated yet horny; I couldn't tell if I was coming or not. I heard myself mewl and sob. My womb fucking *ached*. Why couldn't he get deeper? I needed him deeper. Oh please... Please please please...

"Kirby, look at me." Hugh's command cut through everything. Like I was programmed to obey him instantly.

His mouth was contorted into a snarl, but his eyes were warm. Excited. They bore into mine, deep black pools of lust, and I was drowning in them. He must have hypnotized me—I couldn't look away. I had no idea how I managed to stay on top of the counter because I'd lost sensation in my limbs. My bones rattled around, my muscles too loose to hold me together. Hugh's cock felt massive, but that must have been my hole getting tighter in anticipation.

"Kirby," he mouthed. "Come on. Open up. Let me in, love. Let me in."

He snapped his hips forward, pushing against my closed womb and paused in there for a second before slowly retreating. Another hard thrust. Right there. He set off my orgasm as if he'd hit a light switch.

"Let. Me. In."

"Fuuuck!"

Did I die? Did he kill me with his cock?

His cockhead tore into my core in the middle of my

climax. The pain lasted only a split second because then my womb must have realized that this was what we'd wanted from the start.

I got buried under a fucking avalanche of pleasure. Euphoria. Hugh's eyes got bigger, pitch-black, swallowing me up until I was hidden in the dark, safe and warm, delirious with happiness.

My senses didn't seem to work, but I wasn't afraid. Hugh's cock throbbed in the channel to my womb; his knot grew, locking me to him, and I was perfectly safe.

A blissfully cool sensation blossomed in my center. In the middle of the raging breeding climax, I exhaled with relief, the storm dissolving into delightful flurries and tingles. His cum must have reached my needy womb. Hugh's mouth found mine, and I eagerly let him in. He kissed me deeply, his rumbling moans pouring into me.

An image of a big round belly flashed in my mind, and I could have freaked out. I should be freaking out. But I was too busy savoring the single most beautiful moment of my life.

I'd been bred by many men during my heats, not always because I wanted to. This was different. My womb fell in love with this man's cum, and the pleasure center in my brain turned off everything else. It was just Hugh, filling me up, soaking me with his essence, and tying me to him forever.

Forever.

The wayward word floated around in my mind.

Forever.

But I couldn't dwell on it because suddenly, I was airborne. Impaled as deeply as I could be, still coming on Hugh's knot with the lord of all breeding orgasms, I was flying through the room. Or was I?

Hugh carried me. The rocking movement of his steps enhanced my pleasure, and I clutched at his shoulders. His neck was right there, in front of my mouth, so I bit into it.

"Mmm, my kitty got feral. Yeah. Bite me, love. Fucking suck my blood."

Cool sheets touched my back, and Hugh lay on top of me. He fucked into me, his cockhead pulling on the stretched opening deep inside me, and my eyes rolled back into my head.

"That's it. Gonna fuck you until you pass out. Your womb loves my dick, doesn't it? Want more cum? I'll give you more. Gonna pump you full of it."

Shit. Fucking shit. He was vicious one second and brain-meltingly tender another. I was still coming.

I couldn't move. I heard myself sob but couldn't speak.

"I'm close. Just a little more. You can take it, love. I know you can."

He'd fry my brain.

The climax got hot like lava, and my hole spasmed forcefully. Like a cramp but around Hugh's mammoth knot, and instead of pain, it sent only waves of satisfaction through me. Another cramp. My womb must have pulsated.

Hugh roared and pulled on my hips, burying himself even deeper.

Another splash of cool cum hit the tissue inside my womb, and the sensation pulled me under.

I was floating, hovering in the air, and Hugh held me impaled on the greatest dick of all dicks. Flowers rained on me, the scents heavenly, and I could taste honey on my tongue. No, not honey. Cum. Hugh's cum. It dripped from the flowers like nectar, and I licked my lips, ravenous for it. He thrust into me, and with each fuck, my belly grew under his hands, big and round. I arched in Hugh's arms, feeling overfull, my stomach and chest pulsing and tingling. I'd burst. Disintegrate. I'd fall apart into a million pieces... The pressure rose and rose until I screamed, and my nipples released fountains of white milk.

WHEN I WOKE UP, I was curled up in Hugh's lap like a baby. He half lay, half sat, leaning against a mountain of pillows. Playing with the strand of hair on my forehead, he smiled down at me.

"Hi."

I blinked. My hand drifted to my belly on autopilot. *There.* Fuck, that felt nice.

It's the cum in your womb. But it's never felt like this before?

His hand covered mine.

"Doesn't it hurt?" he asked, his expression anxious. "I couldn't pull out of the mouth to your womb until the knot went down. I'm sorry. You seemed to sleep calmly, but I admit to freaking out a little bit."

I grinned. "I'm not hurt. It feels amazing."

"Yeah?"

I felt my smile widen. "Love your cum in there."

Hugh kissed my nose. "Good." Then his face darkened. "Because Brian wants us to do it in the living room. He wants natural light and ocean view and shit. I'm supposed to breed you on the floor by the bay windows."

On an exhale, I slumped, my happiness slowly drifting away from me.

I couldn't lie to myself anymore. Walter's advice came back to me, clear and so fucking right. Of course I wanted to be alone with Hugh. We should have been alone, just him and me, at my place, hidden from everybody and everything. I wanted him to breed me and kiss me and take care of me, and I wanted the entire world outside our little bubble to go the fuck to hell.

"Okay," I said instead.

He caressed my cheek. "I'm sorry."

I scoffed. "You're sorry? You're the one making this bearable."

He blinked. A flicker of surprise passed over his features, and I realized what I'd said.

"I thought you enjoyed yourself during the films you've made. You've always said that." His tone wasn't accusing, just curious.

That was before I found out how sex could be when you gave a damn about someone.

"I have. You've seen it yourself."

"That one scene, yes."

"I do like it. I'm just tired, I think. And hungry. After how you filled me up this time, I think we might have a little more time. I want a proper meal."

"Sounds brilliant. Come on."

He pushed me into a sitting position and rolled off the bed. Then he handed me my robe.

We walked into the living room and paused by the bay windows. It had snowed outside, and the beach was white, only a ribbon of gray sand lining the gentle waves. The sea was unseasonably calm.

Hugh's phone dinged with a message, and he smiled, reading it. I wondered who it was from but wouldn't ask. An unpleasant thought occurred to me, that he might be dating someone, but no. Hugh was the monogamous type. He wouldn't fuck me during heat and have someone else waiting for him when he was done. Except this wasn't just any heat. This was work. What if—

"It's Jay," he said, still grinning, typing a reply. "The sitter Brian arranged for is good. Monty likes him. But he's asking if I'll be home on Christmas morning."

"Why wouldn't you?"

"I was thinking I'd stay with you for the recovery."

"Oh."

He frowned, searching my face. "I just assumed. Sorry. I...don't have to, obviously. It's just that when you're with someone during heat, you take care of them during recovery, right?"

Right. Of course, Hugh would think it natural.

"But this isn't a normal heat," I said, my voice weak.

He put the phone into the pocket of his bathrobe and walked over to me. Resting his hands on my shoulders, he scrutinized my face with disconcerting focus.

"It's simple, Kirby. You want me to stay, and I'll stay."

I hesitated, my mind reeling. He wouldn't be able to touch me. Why would he want to stay? I'd be just lying around, taking long baths, and moping.

Sensing my hesitation, he smiled encouragingly. "I'll cook for you. We could ask Ilja to send us his goulash recipe. We'll do movie marathons, and later we'll take walks on the beach."

My eyes itched a little, so I blinked a few times. I'd never had anyone taking care of me during recovery except Emerson, and that had been...painful.

Hugh kissed my forehead. "Think about it. You don't have to answer me now."

Just then, Cameron walked in, carrying a tripod and a bundle of rolled-up cables.

"Ignore me. Just setting up."

He placed the tripod on the rug by the bay windows and started unwrapping the cables.

With a grunt and an eye roll, Hugh stepped away.

"Do you want a sandwich, kitten?" he asked, turning to the fridge.

"Sure. What kind of cheese do we have?"

"Cheddar and brie."

"Um..." I mulled it over. I loved both.

"How about I cut the sandwich in half, and you get one piece with cheddar and one with brie?"

I grinned. Having Hugh take care of me during recovery would be fabulous.

CHAPTER 15

HUGH

The light seemed cold, but we were warm and cozy on the fluffy living room carpet. Snowflakes swirled behind the glass wall, the dark waters of the ocean came and went, licking the white beach. Time had slowed down.

Kirby gazed up at me, his eyes catching the hues of the skies outside, dark gray and bottomless. His pupils widened, pinned on me with mindless devotion, and he tilted his head, straining up to me with his parted lips. I kissed him, and his desperate cries quieted.

The greedy mouth to his womb held my cockhead, the sucking sensation it created incredible, like a blowjob within a fuck, and he quaked with his breeding orgasm. My knot pulsated, cum pouring out of my jerking cock in long spurts.

Kirby's heat was peaking, and I was drowning in his pheromones, pleasure coursing through my entire body.

When the climax abated, my knot merely tingling, I rolled onto my back. I expected Kirby to just lie over me like he'd done the last time, but he sat up, bracing himself weakly with his hands in the middle of my chest. He blinked, straightened, and gasped softly. He lifted his hands and caressed his nipples. The expression on his face turned into pure ecstasy. He looked almost drugged. Rolling his hips slowly and tweaking his nipples between his thumbs and forefingers, he threw his head back on a guttural cry. I gripped his hips.

"Careful, kitten," I rasped.

But he didn't listen.

We were locked in breeding, my cockhead was jammed in the channel to his womb, plugging the cum in there, and my knot filled him so much his underbelly bulged when he moved.

He pulled on his nipples, drawing them out until it looked painful, and then he bore down. A piercing shout tore out of his throat. His hard cock twitched above my belly, white cum pearled at the tip and dribbled down onto my skin. I swiped it up and put it into my mouth.

Kirby looked like a freaking demon.

Abusing his nipples, he gyrated his hips and slammed them down, making my cock pierce his core over and over, the mouth to his womb pulling on my cockhead, as if trying to hold me inside. He made beastly sounds, his eyelids drooped, the whites of his eyeballs flashing. Heat cum oozed from his slit in a thin but steady stream.

I slid my hands up to hold his waist. I couldn't stop him, but at least I could support his weight. Pleasure coiled in my balls and knot, another round of release building up...

But suddenly, Kirby swayed, losing all coordination.

"Need more... Need... Hugh. Please!"

He slumped to the side, his hand sliding down the

glass. His hips jerked, but it seemed involuntary. Like he wanted to keep fucking himself but couldn't.

"Need..."

His painful cry spurred me into action. I sat up and hugged him to me. I barely knew how I got there, but in seconds, I was on my knees, holding Kirby by his waist with his legs flung over my arms. His shoulders on the floor, he hung limply in my grip, his body shuddering as I pumped into him. Forget careful. Kirby didn't need careful.

He grappled at the shag carpet with white-knuckled fists, yelling his lungs out. I pulled his entire body onto my knot while I snapped my hips forward, faster and faster, viciously fucking his open womb. And then he went quiet. Eyes closed, mouth slack, body limp, he relaxed in my hold. Only his inner muscles worked overtime, milking my knot, squeezing and quivering, as I came into his core one more time.

Panting, I stilled, letting the pleasure run its course in quiet. I sat on my haunches with Kirby locked to me, his limbs spread like a starfish. I skimmed his splayed body with trembling hands, the curve of his full stomach, his lean thighs, his bloated pecs and reddened nipples. I smeared his cum over his skin, sucking in the powerful scent like an addict. His torso rose and fell with deep breaths, but otherwise, he lay still, eyes closed, a small smile on his lips.

The pair of sneakers by his arm startled me. One almost stepped on his fingers, and Kirby winced, pulling his hand away.

I looked up, glaring daggers at Cameron. "Hey!"

Cameron backed off, but I was already raging inside. I gathered Kirby into my arms, tucking his face into the crook of my neck, holding him by his back and nape.

"Hugh... I'm thirsty," Kirby whispered.

"We need a break," I said, turning to Brian.

Except he made a zip over his mouth and gestured for me to continue.

Continue what?

Kirby was out of it. What more did they want?

"Turn it all off," I said, my voice rising. "Now."

Brian rolled his eyes and threw his arms in the air, exasperated. But he still didn't say anything to the crew. Cameron walked around us with the gear, objective aimed at Kirby's limp form, while Trent hid behind the stationary camera. I tightened my hold on Kirby, keeping his face hidden from them.

"Turn it off!" I yelled.

"Guys, turn it off," Brian said. He looked fuming. "What the hell, Hugh?"

Cameron finally walked away from us, which calmed me down somewhat.

"Kirby needs something to drink. Bring me a water bottle and orange juice."

"You can't decide when a scene ends, Hugh. That's my job."

"Bring me the fucking drinks, Brian!" Okay, I wasn't calm. Not at all. My omega had all but fainted in my lap, my swollen cock was up his womb, and there were people in the room, yapping at us. The alpha in me was furious.

Brian pushed off his chair and walked over to the bar. He brought a glass of juice with a straw and a water bottle. I held the glass to Kirby's lips, and he found the straw, gulping the juice gratefully. Then I gave him the water to wash it down.

"We're going to talk about this, Hugh."

I didn't respond to Brian's remark. "Blanket."

He handed me the fleece, and I wrapped it around Kirby's motionless body. On my butt and one hand, I shuffled over to a corner and leaned against the wall. My back felt cold, but Kirby was safely tucked to me, covered in a fluffy blanket, emanating heat, so I could easily ignore my own discomfort.

The crew was almost done picking up their shit, so I closed my eyes, trying to mentally erase them.

"As soon as you're done here, we need to talk," Brian said again.

I didn't reply.

Three pairs of feet shuffled away, and I nuzzled Kirby's forehead. He was deeply asleep.

My knot took almost an hour to recede. I carefully pulled out and gathered Kirby to my chest. Groaning, I stood and carried him to the bedroom. He didn't even stir. I tucked him in, bunching up the duvet around him. He looked safe, curled up in a little nest of pillows, so I took a swift shower and pulled on a pair of sweats.

Then I went back to the living room. Brian was already there, typing something on his tablet.

Folding my arms over my chest, I waited for him to get it out. I knew what he was going to say.

"It's the middle of the heat, and your instincts are all over the place. I understand that. But you don't get to yell commands during a scene."

"Kirby needed a break."

Brian glared up at me. "I needed thirty more seconds, Hugh. I saw that Kirby was exhausted, but I needed to see him lean against you and relax so I could have had a natural closing clip for the scene. Then I would have told the guys to wrap it up and helped you to take care of him. Only thirty more seconds. Except you started yelling."

I blinked. Had I fucked up?

"I'm an omega, Hugh. I've been through heats myself, and I've filmed quite a few. I can see and hear when Kirby needs something just like you can. But we have work to do here. Work that you get very well paid for. I took my chances with you, convincing everyone involved that despite being an amateur, you could pull this off. Don't let me down this close to the finish line."

"Cameron almost stepped on his hand," I protested weakly.

"And I can see how that set you off. I get it. But next time, you're going to trust me."

Clenching my fists, I tried to think around my anger. Was he right? Had I overreacted?

"Look, Hugh, you're protective of Kirby, and that's only natural. It's what I wanted to happen with this film. You have developed a connection that makes the sex look magical. And I also understand how such a connection makes it difficult for you to remain calm." He pointed a finger at me, pinning me with his clever eyes. "But you will show me some fucking respect. I care about Kirby too. He's not only my best-earning star, but I consider him my friend. I'm doing an excellent job of making this entire production a pleasant and safe experience for him. You're going to act professional, listen to your director, and we're going to film another breeding scene in the same spot with the next wave. The cameras stay on until I say otherwise."

I had overreacted. But what did Brian expect?

"Tell Cameron to watch his fucking feet," I muttered.

"Already done. Anything else?"

"I need to get back to Kirby."

"You do that. For the next wave, bring him here."

"That can be in a few hours already."

"Then you better go take a nap."

I huffed. The annoyance didn't abate, not even a little. On a rational level, I did understand Brian's perspective. I really did. But my alpha wanted to grab his omega and hide him away where nobody could find us until Kirby was safely recovered.

I left Brian there without another word and hurried back to Kirby. He hadn't moved, luckily not noticing I'd been gone.

He felt so warm and soft against me, smelling sweetly of dry slick and heat cum. I buried my nose in the soft hair at his nape and closed my eyes, trying to forget about the outside world for a few minutes.

CHAPTER 16

KIRBY

I wasn't sure what was real and what was a dream, but it didn't matter. I could sense Hugh by my side at all times, asleep or awake, so I knew I was safe. My hole felt full, but my womb ached with emptiness, and I searched Hugh's face for clues as to what was happening. I wasn't afraid. Just curious.

We were on the beach, in the snow, but it didn't feel cold or wet. The ocean hummed quietly, and Hugh smiled down at me. He cupped my jaw, caressing my lips with his thumb, and I pulled it into my mouth. I liked sucking on it. The unpleasant emptiness abated, giving way to a glorious explosion of raw pleasure, and I tightened my lips around Hugh's thumb. My stomach felt warm, and I closed my eyes with the blissful sensation. On some level, I was aware of my own movements—I pushed onto his cock, meeting his furious fucks, making his cockhead slide through the channel to my womb because the fierce orgasm it brought was like a drug for me. But I couldn't control my body. It moved how it wanted, driven by some hidden part of my brain, primitive and reckless.

"Shh. I got you. I know."

He fucked me even harder, and I slumped with relief. I needed him to impale me through and through, to punch into my womb, stretch it and tear it so it finally stopped hurting with hunger.

Then it happened. The cooling balm filled me in pulses, soaking me on the inside. The fresh load of Hugh's cum in my womb brought me complete ecstasy of body and mind.

I could finally relax. With both hands on my belly, I caressed the spot where Hugh poured his cum into me. The best thing, he kept coming. My sense of time was nonexistent, but it felt like ages. Hugh's knot throbbed against my gland, his cockhead lurched in my core, and another wave of pleasure spread from my womb where his cum coated the overheated tissue. After a few heartbeats, it happened again. He caressed my body, kissed my face, holding me securely in his lap, and our climax rose and withdrew and rose again like the tide.

His fingers tangled in my hair, and his lips brushed my forehead. I wanted to hug him but couldn't move.

"Want to...hold you."

My alpha understood. He always understood. He brought my arms up around his neck, and I relaxed, content like never before in my life. I was safe.

I must have slept for a while because the next thing I knew, we were on the sofa and I was covered in blankets. I was still knotted in Hugh's lap, breathing in the musky, sweaty scent of his skin, but he must have pulled out of my womb.

"Hugh."

"Hi, kitten. How are you?"

"Mmm, happy." The room swayed a little, blurry. Was there mist inside? But I was warm, so it didn't matter if it snowed right on top of my head. Hugh would keep me warm.

"Me too." Another kiss to my forehead.

"Where are they?" Did Brian leave?

"Done for now. You can rest."

"I want them gone." Hugh would take care of me. I didn't need anybody else. I didn't want anybody but my alpha with me. He tilted my face back with his broad hand. His eyes searched mine. God, he was beautiful.

"You're so gorgeous." I sounded a little strange, but he could hear me. He got it. My alpha always understood me even when I couldn't speak at all. My alpha held me and kept me warm. He protected me. "I'm so happy it's you. I wish you could get me pregnant."

Hugh smiled, looking a little sad. "You don't even want kids."

"I know." I didn't want a baby. But I liked the idea of being impregnated by him. If his seed took root inside me, then he'd keep me, right? He wouldn't leave me. Maybe there was some other way to stay connected to him.

I couldn't go back to being cold and alone. Hugh was now a part of me, tied to me by an invisible rope, right here in my middle. If it tore, it would gut me.

"You're sleepy, kitten. You should rest some more."

I nuzzled his jaw, rubbing my face against his stubble. "I love your cum in my womb. Feels so fucking good. It's making me so happy."

"I'm glad. Because I love pumping you full of it."

I love you. "I want them all gone, Hugh. I want to make love just you and me."

Hugh groaned and kissed me. I felt the kiss all the way

to my core. He tasted so good, felt so good. I was bathing in his scent, full of his cum, and it felt like nobody else had ever touched me before. Nobody would after. Hugh wouldn't allow it. I belonged to him now.

"Me too, my love," he whispered against my lips. "I want to hide you away and keep you."

"I wish you could do that. Keep me. You're the best, Hugh. Nobody's ever made me feel this good. I wish you could make them all go away and keep me."

The room was getting dark, and Hugh's beautiful face seemed to be glowing.

"Kirby, baby, you're half asleep. Rest."

"I mean it. I want you to teach me." Did I slur? Did he understand? It was vital that he knew I meant it.

"Teach you what, love?"

"Making love. You know how to do it, but I don't. I only know how to fuck." His face was disappearing into the darkness. I was so, so tired. "Make them all go away, Hugh, please. I want to make love for real. I don't want it to be pretend."

"It's not. We are making love for real."

"Stay here. In me."

"Not going anywhere, my little kitten."

CHAPTER 17

HUGH

Kirby had these periods of half-consciousness when he seemed to be dreaming with his eyes open. It usually happened during and after a breeding orgasm. It scared me at first, but both Brian and later Walter, whom I'd insisted on calling, assured me that it was normal and safe.

"It's fine, Hugh," Kirby said. "I'm having the time of my life."

"Do you even remember it?"

"Not really, but that's okay. I remember feeling happy."

It was the sixth day, and the intensity was supposed to ebb now. Kirby was awake and seemed content enough. He downed a protein shake, and I helped him to the bathroom. He was shaky but alert.

"Could you close the door, please?" he said, standing above the toilet with his eyebrows raised.

"Oh, sorry." I backed out of the bathroom and waited, sitting on the bed. Anxiously, I listened for an ominous thump in case he fell, but the toilet flushed, water ran through the pipes, and then the sound of the shower came through the door.

Was he showering without me?

I stood and marched to the door. "Can I join you?" I yelled.

"Sure."

I exhaled with relief and went in, dropping my robe onto the floor. Stepping under the spray, I plastered myself to Kirby's naked body and took the shower gel from him. He giggled.

"Separation anxiety? My poor alpha man. The heat is screwing with your head, isn't it?"

I harrumphed and covered his lean back in suds.

"It's okay. It screws with mine, too. I don't remember half of yesterday. I kept dreaming we were fucking on the beach in the snow."

I did remember. Every word.

Make them all go away, Hugh, please. I want to make love for real.

He did want that, just like me. He was just convinced he couldn't have it, so he would never have voiced it out loud if he hadn't been affected by the peaking heat. But he did mean it. He must have meant it.

The love we could have hovered just within our grasp. We had to make it through this absurd, twisted setup, and then I'd tell him. We'd figure it out together.

Holding him with his back to my chest, I nuzzled his hair and massaged his front, soaping up his soft cock and balls. He hummed, leaning against me.

"I feel it coming again," he murmured. "We should get out."

I groaned. "Do we have to tell them? Can't we skip one round? I'll knot you in here, and nobody needs to know."

But Kirby stepped away and reached for the towel. He hastily rubbed it down his body and threw it on top of my robe.

"Hurry up," he called over his shoulder.

The distant beeping sound came through the walls—he'd hit the panic button.

When I returned to the bedroom, Trent and Brian were already there. The scent of another heatwave was thick in the air. Kirby lay on his side on the bed, his eyes on me. He gave me a half-smile, sad and tired, and I wanted to smash all the equipment and drag the crew out of there. Why couldn't I make love to my mate like a normal person?

You wanted this, remember?

"We're rolling," Brian announced.

"Fisting time," Kirby said and winked, zapping my brain.

Fuck. Fisting. I could do that.

I knelt by the bed, gripped Kirby's ankles and pulled him to me. He laughed, but then his laughter died down when I latched onto his swollen pucker with my mouth. He was so soft, like silk and honey, and the juices he was leaking were getting better and better. His hole fluttered around my tongue, and he moaned.

With the camera over my shoulder, I pushed two fingers inside him. He was so loose it barely stretched him. I used two fingers from each hand and pulled his hole open, and he groaned.

"Oh yeah. Fuck, yeah. I can't wait for your hand."

The heat wave was getting stronger by the second. Kirby's muscles quivered as he held his legs open with his arms hooked under his knees. His body gaped around my fingers, and with a shiver, his hole released an excess of slick. It ran down my hands, so I pushed my fingers in and out, smearing it over my knuckles.

"Deeper," Kirby cried. "Oh please, deeper!"

His wails weren't for the cameras. I could feel the need in his trembling flesh. The heat wave was quickly turning into a tsunami.

I pulled the fingers of my left hand out and spread the slick over my right. Then I tucked my thumb into my palm and pushed four fingers into Kirby's opening.

His answering cry was full of excitement and anticipation. He truly wanted this, and his need for me made the rest okay. Kirby needed this, and I could forget about the crew for a while.

I pumped my hand in and out, deeper on each thrust, until Kirby's wet rim touched the knuckles of my fist. It seemed impossible, but when I stilled and pushed a little, rotating my hand, I was able to get in even deeper.

"More. More!" Kirby sounded desperate. "Shove it in. I can take it. Please, just shove it in."

It looked so violent. His pink flesh exposed, my hand stretching him open, my fist so thick compared to his pale, skinny ass...

"Harder!" Kirby shrieked, and I pushed.

His rim slid down to my wrist like a glove. Shit, he felt so fucking soft. Hot and pliant and *soft*.

His inner muscles contracted around my hand, and he came, his cum flying in an arch and splattering onto his chest. His yelling sounded euphoric.

My Kirby needed this.

I pumped my hand, his rim gliding over my wrist, back and forth, and farther still, where my forearm got thicker. My hand bathed in the abundance of slick. It felt so dangerously easy. My entire fucking arm stuck out of Kirby's body. It looked so wrong, but he kept coming.

Then I found it.

The protruding mouth to his womb touched my fingertips, and the bump of eager flesh pulsated. I burrowed my middle finger into the center, just the tip, and wiggled it.

Kirby screamed, his legs and arms twitching, and I remembered what he'd said in the session with Walter. I took his cock down my throat and sucked, gulping his delicious cum.

His hole kept clenching, the mouth to his womb shivering against my fingers, but Kirby went limp on the bed, letting go of his legs. Spreadeagled, he lay there and took it, his groans guttural.

His cock jerked in my mouth, but his orgasm had gone dry. When he got hoarse, I relented. Slowly, I pulled my hand out. Before Kirby could protest, I shoved the prepared dildo into him and inflated the artificial knot with a few pumps of my hand.

He sighed with relief.

"Hugh," he murmured, stretching his arms toward me weakly.

I climbed onto the bed, and Kirby curled into me. I didn't get what he was after until his mouth wrapped around my cockhead. Humming, he suckled while massaging the base, and I lost it way too soon.

My cock swelled in his hand, and he swallowed my cum. My knot ached, the skin stretched uncomfortably, like it would burst, and I let out an undignified whine. I got it now, why some people hated knotting into thin air. But Kirby knew. He kept kneading it, soothing the ache, and I spurted into his mouth a few more times, my skin prickling all over. I couldn't decide if it was too much or not enough, but the sight of him like that, taking care of my knot, was out of this world. He suckled on it, stroking my cock, and I weaved my slick-stained fingers into his hair. He looked like a hungry animal, licking me and rubbing his face against me. He glanced up, his mouth parted, tongue circling around the knot, then he took it into his mouth, barely able to wrap his lips around the bulge. His eyes rolled back into his head.

When he sucked hard on the knot and squeezed my balls, I roared from the overload of sensation. My cum bubbled up, oozing from my slit and dripping onto Kirby's face. Kirby gripped the knot in his fist, holding it tight, and caught the next spurt into his mouth.

After I stopped shuddering, he settled with his head on my thigh and suckled on my cock, holding the knot with both hands. His eyes closed. Would he fall asleep like this?

Staring at him in awe, I barely noticed when the crew turned their shit off and left.

When the knot went down, I gathered Kirby into my arms and gently removed the toy from his ass. He sighed.

"Your cum tastes delicious," he murmured against my chest. "Love sucking you. Why can't I suck you while you knot me? That would have been ideal."

"Because I only have one cock?"

He giggled. "Pity. You could have one more dick growing out of your hand or something, and it would shoot cum into my mouth while you fucked me. You'd be my ideal man."

I laughed. "You're crazy."

"Mhmm. I know."

He tilted his face up and kissed me. Was he aware he acted like my lover even when the cameras were off? Did he act like this with his other co-stars? I refused to believe it.

His glistening eyes held mine, and he smiled, a little sad but content, too.

"You're great, Hugh. Thank you for everything."

A vague plan was forming in my head, a little insane but so right. I needed to know for sure he wanted the same, though.

"You really don't remember last night?" I asked and held my breath.

"Just bits and pieces."

"You said you wished the crew was gone."

"Yeah." He looked down, hiding his tender eyes from me. "But it is what it is." He shrugged one shoulder.

I threw my arm around him and pulled him to me, and he nuzzled my chest. "I love touching you," I whispered. "Being inside you is the best feeling on earth. I don't regret a thing."

"I love it too. It's been my best heat."

Considering what he'd been through, the compliment fell flat. I didn't want his praise. I wanted him to be happy. Truly, deeply happy.

"Thank you, Hugh. I mean it. I didn't think I was able to let go and savor sex this much. But you make me feel so good, my head empties out, and I can just drift through the heat waves on cloud nine."

"Don't thank me," I said, my voice a bit shaky. Guilt nagged at me, but I couldn't even tell what I'd done wrong.

His lips brushed my collarbone. "Love fucking you." There was a teasing smile in his voice, so I swallowed the lump in my throat and held him.

At least I now had a plan. I knew what I had to do to get a chance with my boy.

. . .

KIRBY HUGGED the pillow I'd slept on, and I dragged the covers higher up until only his nose was peeking out. Then I snuck out of the bedroom.

I found Brian on the ground floor in his home studio. He and Trent were going through the footage from yesterday. When I knocked, he stood up and exited the room to join me in the hall.

"Is something the matter?" he asked, a worried frown on his forehead.

"Can we talk?"

"Sure."

"Upstairs. I need to be close to Kirby in case he wakes up." I was itching to go back.

"Of course." He stuck his head back into the studio. "Trent, take a break."

Brian and I took the stairs, and he was uncharacteristically quiet. Did he somehow sense what I wanted to talk about?

We sat down in the living room, and I grabbed a bottle of water, mostly to have something to play with while I tiptoed through the possibly most precarious conversation of my life.

"I have a huge favor to ask you."

"I'm all ears," he said, giving me an unsure smile.

"You chose me for this film because you wanted someone real. Someone who could form a genuine connection with Kirby."

"Yes. And I don't regret my choice. You've been amazing, both of you. The material we have is outstanding."

I wrinkled my nose. "I, um, have done what you wanted. Formed a connection." I lifted my eyes to meet Brian's quick gaze. "I love Kirby. I've loved him for a while now, but the heat of course...made things more intense."

I waited for him to say something, but he didn't. He just watched me, unsurprised. Of course he wasn't surprised. He'd seen me make love to Kirby. He knew what I felt maybe better than I did.

I gulped. "I think Kirby feels the same."

"I think so too." Brian smiled encouragingly.

"When we were alone, he asked me. No. He hinted at it. At being alone with me for the heat."

Brian frowned, but I plowed forward. I had nothing to lose.

"He's never had that, Brian. His entire sex life has been either abuse or this." I waved my hand around in the air, and before Brian could get defensive, I continued. "And you've helped him so much. Getting him to talk to Walter, choosing his co-stars, making sure he was safe and could feel pleasure on set. He's grateful to you and respects you immensely. I do, too."

"What do you want me to do, Hugh?" Brian asked, sounding tired.

"I want to ask you to wrap up. Leave us alone for the last three days."

Brian glared at me. "Not such an exhibitionist after all, are you?"

"The thought of people seeing me knot Kirby does excite me. Not gonna lie. But this is more important than some kink. I need to take care of him, make him happy, and the shoot is exhausting him not just physically but emotionally."

Leaning back into the sofa, Brian exhaled loudly. He didn't say anything. Which was a good sign, right?

"He's never had a private, loving sexual encounter in his life, Brian. I don't think he knows he could have it. That it would feel different."

"Does he know you're talking to me about this?"

I shook my head. "He asked to be alone with me, but that was when he was out of it after a breeding."

Brian's eyebrows flew up. "Come again?"

"The dreamlike trance he sometimes fell into. He talked when it happened on the fifth day. I can't repeat exactly what he said because that would be betraying his trust."

"I understand."

"The point is, I know he wants it. To be left in peace for once in his life. Just for a few days. To be vulnerable in private. To allow himself to feel."

He smirked. "And you want to be his hero?"

"Well, yeah." I let out a broken laugh. "I want him happy. So I'm doing what I think will make him happy. Walter says it's my alpha trait, enhanced during my partner's heat. I'm caring and protective, he says. So, I'm embracing it. I want to take care of Kirby. Alone."

Folding his arms over his chest, Brian regarded me coolly. "Do you have any idea how much money we have riding on this wild horse?"

"But you already have everything, don't you? You've sat in that little room every waking hour when we weren't filming. You have hours and hours of footage, all of it, from wild fucking to Kirby asleep and defenseless. You don't need more. Not really."

His mouth tightened, his eyes still wary. He hadn't decided. Which was good. Great even.

"You say he's your friend. That you care about him as a person, not just as a million-dollar ass."

Brian pointed a finger at me. "Emotional blackmail will get you nowhere."

I bit my lip. "Sorry."

He shook his head, his gaze wandering around.

"I love him, Brian."

"And you need to go back to him." He rubbed his hands down his face and shook his head, obviously frustrated with me. We weren't friends, and I couldn't rely on him doing what I wanted just because I asked him to. But he was an omega, a compassionate one, and he genuinely cared about Kirby. Biting my tongue before I annoyed him even more, I waited.

After a while, Brian stood, rolling his shoulders.

"You so owe me, Urban," he groused. "You so fucking owe me. You both do."

I grinned. I hadn't really believed I could convince him. *Wow*.

"Thank you."

Brian threw me a lethal glare. "We'll do an interview after recovery, and you'll fucking spill your heart out on camera for me. And you'll do the promotional tour without a single whine, event after event, or I'll sue your ass black-and-blue, get it?"

"Yes, boss. I'm your slave. Whatever you say."

"Get out of my sight before I change my mind."

I hopped up, high on adrenaline. "Kirby's still asleep. I don't think a shotgun would wake him up now. Can we..."

Brian rolled his eyes. "I'll call Trent."

CHAPTER 18

KIRBY

I woke up feeling warm and gooey. I wasn't sure I could move, but when I tried to wriggle, it wasn't so bad. The dull ache in my lower back signaled another heat wave within minutes, but it didn't feel as urgent as before. I groaned, and Hugh's hold on me tightened.

"Can you reach the button?" I mumbled, unwilling to move just yet.

"No need."

He must have smelled the heat wave coming and had already signaled for Brian. In no time, they'd be here. I opened my eyes, taking slow breaths, willing my body to cooperate. I was so exhausted. I wished I could just roll over onto my belly, spread my legs, and Hugh could have his way with me while I'd take a nap.

Hugh ran his hand down my arm. His erection poked my ass cheeks, and fresh slick was already gathering in my hole. Yes, I was longing for the filming to be over, but at least I'd get to feel Hugh in me a few more times.

Something didn't seem right, though.

What was taking Brian so long?

"You did push the panic button, didn't you?"

"No."

Startled, I sat up, looking around the suddenly unfamiliar room.

"Where's the gear? Are we supposed to do another scene in the living room or bathroom?" I wasn't keen on another wave in awkward, acrobatic positions on a hard-ass floor.

But everything was gone. *Everything.* The bedroom was empty aside from a lone black extension cord on the floor and a couple of folding chairs leaning against the wall in the corner.

Hugh caught my hand and tugged me down on the bed. Confused, I turned to face him.

"What's going on?"

He looked sheepish. "It's finished. They don't need to film anymore."

"What?"

"The crew packed and left when you were asleep."

"Brian said we're done?" My stomach heaved. Did I fuck up somehow after all? "Did he cancel the project?"

"No. He has all the footage he needs."

The ache in my lower back bloomed, the warmth getting harder to ignore, but my mind still spun.

"We're alone?" The question came as a whisper.

Hugh cupped my cheek, his eyes so tender I felt a responding stab in my chest. "You wanted it to be over, so I asked Brian, and he agreed. Is that okay?"

"Yes, it's fucking okay." I blew out a startled laugh. "You convinced Brian to wrap up early? It's just us? For the rest of the heat?" Was I dreaming this?

"Yeah. We can stay here until the recovery is over. Brian says hi and to order food on his account."

Hugh's fingers danced along my jaw and down the side of my neck. He seemed a little worried but excited, too.

We were alone.

I was alone with Hugh. For days. In bed.

The heat wave began with a flutter in my inner muscles and a throb in my cock. Now that Brian wasn't here to give instructions, I didn't know what to do. How did Hugh want me? Should I...suck him for a bit and ride him? Or did he want me on my knees?

"I..."

But before I could ask, he leaned in to kiss me. His hand drifted to my hip, and he rolled us so he was on top of me. Automatically, I spread my legs and lifted them, offering him my body. He didn't even break the kiss as he stuffed a pillow under my ass and guided his erection into me. He filled me with a slow thrust, his cockhead pressing against the mouth to my womb, and I moaned into the kiss.

Then he did something that blew my mind.

He dragged the duvet over us. He covered us.

Just enough light made it in around the duvet for me to discern Hugh's tender smile. He cradled my face in his big, warm hands and rocked slowly, his gaze searching mine and his thick cock sliding through my tingling flesh. He kissed my nose, then bumped the tip with his. "Is this okay, kitten? I want to go slow. I want to savor you."

Mute, I nodded. For some stupid reason, my eyes itched. I closed them, and Hugh peppered kisses all over my face, including my eyelids.

We were covered. Hidden. It didn't matter how we looked.

It doesn't matter how it looks.

The sensations grew in force, and I shivered, inexplicably scared. What was I afraid of? Not of Hugh, no.

I whimpered, and Hugh thrust harder, his cockhead breaching the mouth to my womb. After so many breedings, it was easy. The channel swallowed him up, and my orgasm flared from the spot, deliciously slow and powerful, chasing all fears away.

Gasping against Hugh's lips, I let ecstasy take over.

He didn't knot me right away. He fucked my open womb, in and out, making me come in waves. I was hidden in his arms and under the covers, safe like in a blanket fort, and he kissed me again, his tongue finding mine.

At some point, the tears must have leaked out of the corners of my eyes.

Hugh slowed down even more, just rocking us gently, his cockhead only kissing the loose opening in my core. "Kirby, baby, what is it?"

I shook my head. "Nothing. Don't stop."

He pushed in again, and I gave out a low cry. "Kirby?"

"It's beautiful. Don't stop. Breed me, please. It's so good."

He sipped the tears from my temples, then thrust harder. I could tell by his growling moans that he was close.

"Breed me, Hugh. Do it."

"Kirby..."

Groaning, he braced himself up on his hands by my shoulders, and the duvet slid down, bunching up around his hips. He buried himself deep, breaching me all the way. His muscles bulged under my fingers as I held on to his arms. My climax stormed through me while his knot stretched me out too fast, and it could have gotten uncomfortable, but his cum flooded my womb and made everything right.

Hugh lowered himself on top of me and captured my lips again. His cock lurched in my core, releasing more seed, and we both moaned into the kiss.

For once, I was perfectly awake. Sane.

I was aware of everything, every single tendril of pleasure, everywhere we touched, the gentle flicks of his tongue and his hot breaths. The scent of our bodies and heat cum burned through my lungs, strong after we sweated under the duvet, and I wanted to rub it all into my skin so I could smell of our sex forever.

"The little mouth up your hole, it suckles on my cock. Do you feel it? Feel my cum filling you up?"

"Yes. Love it. Love your cum."

We were alone.

My hand shook when I lifted it to his nape. It was so confusing. Physically, I felt better than ever before, but in my head, it was chaos. My alpha bred me, and I belonged to him. I was joined with him, just him and me, and I loved it. He hid me from the world, covered me and protected me, and I was safer than ever. Cherished.

Except it wasn't real. Or was it? The cameras were gone. Could it be real now?

Hugh turned onto his back, bringing me with him, and the duvet wrapped around us like a cocoon. With the motion, Hugh's cockhead popped out of the channel to my womb. One last orgasm fizzled through me, brief and sweet, and I slumped over his chest. His hands painted circles on my lower back, the sheets whispering around us. The warmth was delicious.

"They're gone." Did I say it out loud?

"Yeah."

Did we just...make love? Was this how it felt? And why the fuck was I still crying?

"Kirby, did I do something wrong? I should have asked you before I went to Brian, shouldn't I?"

I shook my head. I couldn't speak, or my voice would break.

"Are you okay, kitten?"

I nodded, smearing the tears into his skin.

"Oh baby," he sighed and cupped my head. He held me while I wept, barely knowing why. I was happy—he'd just filled my womb, his knot still held us together, and my body hummed with contentment.

"Thank you, Hugh," I managed after a while, a little hoarse. "I'm great. I really am. No idea why I'm crying."

He tilted my face back, his thumb stroking my chin. I let him. He'd seen me at my worst already, so there was no point in hiding my tears.

"You said you wanted them gone, and I had to give it to you. Just had to."

"You wanted to show me how it could be." And fuck, I wanted it too. I ached for it. "To make love."

He gave me a small smile. "Can I?"

Swallowing the lump in my throat, I smiled back. "Yes. It's what we're doing right now, isn't it?"

"Yes. I think so." He sighed, thumbs brushing my jaw. "I'll take care of you, Kirby. I'll make it good."

"I trust you."

He kissed and caressed me until the knot went down, then he carried me to the shower. He opened my ass with his fingers to help the cum and slick run out. Covered in suds, I stood leaning on the wall while he massaged my pecs, ass, and thighs. After drying me head to toe, he wrapped me in the bathrobe. When I needed to pee, he turned with his back to me to brush his teeth but didn't go away, and the familiarity of it fucked with my head further.

Wearing only the terrycloth robes, we lounged in the living room, and Hugh made us something fizzy with next to no alcohol. It tasted fruity, reminding me of the long, lazy evenings at the pub in the summer with Hugh, Emerson, and Burke. We ate cheese and crackers, listened to low music, and just looked at the view.

Wind howled outside, the skies dark gray, and I didn't even know what time it was. The ocean roared today, high waves rising and crashing, but we were cozied up under a fleece blanket on the sofa.

I fell asleep for a while, and when I woke up, I was cuddled to Hugh's chest. I could sense he was awake, but he sat still, his nose in my hair, hands on my neck, and naked ass under the bathrobe. I didn't move either, didn't say anything. I just breathed him in and soaked up his warmth.

Another heat wave came creeping, unhurried but still forceful, and I straddled Hugh where we were, taking his cock to the hilt on the first thrust, all the way to my open, fucked-out womb. He held my hips in a firm grip and fucked up into me as I bore down. He bred me deeply, making me shout, and I shook in his arms, overwhelmed but so fucking happy.

"Don't pull out of there," I mumbled, hoping he'd understand.

He locked his arms around me, holding me impaled until he softened inside me.

Half-asleep, I hugged his neck as he carried me to bed, and as soon as he laid me down on the rumpled covers in our little nest that still smelled like sex, my hands went to my belly. I stroked the spot where his cum remained in me, and my mind wandered, stuck in a strange, dreamlike trance.

I belonged to Hugh. He'd bred me, so I was his. I even smelled like him, and everybody would know. It was as if I had it tattooed on my forehead now and branded into my heart. I wasn't my own person anymore. I belonged to Hugh.

The toilet flushed, water ran in the sink in the bathroom, and he came back. Scared, I met his gaze. Did he feel it? Did he know? Because I couldn't be without him. I'd bleed out.

"Hey, kitten. Come here."

He gestured to his chest, and I plastered myself to him, kissing his skin where I could reach.

My alpha. He wouldn't leave me. He'd take care of me.

"Mmm. You're sweet, baby. So sweet. My darling boy."

I wouldn't cry again. I was happy.

Was I dreaming? The world seemed a little blurry around the edges, but Hugh was solid, his eyes sharp as ever. Maybe it was the heat, but somehow, I knew what I was feeling was bigger than that. It ran deeper than anything I'd ever felt before, and it would not just disappear again. I was changed.

CHAPTER 19

HUGH

I thought three days would be plenty if we spent every hour together, but time seemed to pass way too quickly. Kirby had seven more heat waves, gradually milder and longer apart, and I cherished every opportunity to make love to him. I spooned him on the bed, breeding him early on and then fucking him with the knot. He wouldn't say it, but it was obvious how much he liked being held like that. He would crane his neck so we could kiss while I moved inside him, and he'd clutch my forearms over his chest. He got so pliant and mellow afterward, smiling sleepily and kissing my hands, playing with my fingers. Then I took him face to face, holding his legs to his chest and making him wail with impatience before I bred him. When I filled his womb with my cum, his eyes got big, pupils blown, and he murmured sweet nonsense, delirious with pleasure.

Kirby looked half-asleep most of the time, his eyes unguarded and vulnerable, and the alpha in me ached with the overload of tenderness I felt for my boy. When he cried, even though he claimed those were happy tears, my chest hurt. I hugged and kissed him at breakfast, and my snarky boy's eyes welled up once more.

"I'm an emotional wreck."

"It's the heat."

"Yeah. Sure."

He wiped his face with the back of his hand. I dragged my chair to his side and sat shoulder to shoulder with him.

"The eggs are good?" I asked. I wouldn't poke and pry when he was at his most vulnerable. He'd tell me what the matter was when he was ready.

"They're great. I can't cook for shit."

Of course he couldn't. He spent his teenage years out on the streets. "I can teach you."

He looked up at me. "Yeah?"

"Sure. Cooking together is great fun. And now when the heat is fading, we'll have time."

"Okay. I'd like that."

He rested his head on my shoulder while I drank my coffee.

"I'm not crying because I'm sad," he said after a while.

"I think I get it."

"I mean, I am a little sad but not because of what's happening now."

I put my arm around his back. "You're sad because of what happened to you in the past."

He shrugged. "I guess."

After another minute of silence, he brushed his hand over my thigh. "I wonder how it would have been if I was someone else. Had a different life. Maybe I'd have met you, and we'd have gone out on a date. Like normal people."

"We can do that. I'd love to take you out on a date."

He let out a half-laugh half-sigh but didn't reply.

. . .

THE NEXT DAY, we made love around noon. The heat wave was slow, Kirby's scent faint.

"It's the last one, isn't it?" he asked when I knotted him.

I wrapped myself around him, staying deep inside his body, my cockhead pressed up against his now sealed womb.

"It seems so."

He turned his head so he could kiss me. My knot receded way too soon. Kirby rolled in my arms and hugged me, hiding his face in the crook of my neck. Was he saying goodbye? In a few hours, he'd go into the recovery stage and wouldn't tolerate my touch. Any touch.

I'd successfully avoided thinking about it, but our expiration date was here. Now.

"Kirby, I'm staying, okay?"

He nodded, rubbing his face against my throat. "Not like I can bear the thought of you leaving," he mumbled into my skin. He sounded resentful, like he didn't want to depend on me, but even so, his admission made me happy.

"Good. Because they would have to drag me away."

He chuckled humorlessly. For a while, we just lay there, quiet. Kirby turned onto his back. "What's happened to us?"

I propped myself on my arm so I could look at him. He glared at the ceiling lamp like he found something offending about it.

"Don't you know, kitten?"

He flashed me a startled look like I'd surprised him by pointing out the elephant in the room. Then he rolled off the bed and stood.

"I need to pee," he mumbled without looking at me.

When the bathroom door closed behind him, I sighed. I just needed to be patient with him, and I was already damned good at that. Just a little more time. After all these years, I could wait for a few more days and let him recover in peace. When he was ready, he'd just need to reach out, and I'd be right here with as much love as he could carry.

With his hair wet from the shower, he emerged a few minutes later, wrapped in a bathrobe. He scowled at nothing in particular.

"I'm sore already."

"I'm sorry. This part sucks, I know. How about I make you dinner and a couple of drinks?"

"Do you know how to make mac and cheese?"

I sat up, grinning at his choice of a dish. "Of course. I live with an nine-year-old, remember?"

"Can you teach me?"

"Sure. Let me just take a quick shower."

"Okay."

Kirby grated all the cheese and observed everything I did with a cute, focused frown on his forehead. Feeding him would never cease to fascinate me. He treated each dish almost like a religious experience, starting out slowly and carefully, tasting the first bit, then humming with closed eyes and nodding to himself.

"This is amazing. The ones I buy never taste like this. So creamy. Yum."

I bit my tongue so I wouldn't laugh. At the same time, knowing why he appreciated the simplest stuff so much made me bone-deep sad.

After Kirby had eaten, he slept for ages, until noon the next day. Despondent and exhausted, he spent the rest of the day wrapped in blankets in front of the TV. I fed him and generally just hovered. To my great relief, he still wanted to sleep in the same bed. I kept tossing and turning, but his silhouette in the dark was my anchor.

Some part of me must have known already that Kirby loved me because the waiting didn't feel so daunting anymore. The recovery made him distant, but I knew it had nothing to do with me. What I hated was watching him suffer.

Hot water seemed to be the trick. When Kirby got miserable, he took a long hot shower. It helped with the soreness and stiff muscles, and it seemed to soothe him even emotionally. Food was another remedy. Kirby had an admirable appetite, especially for anything containing cheese, butter, or cream, and I loved indulging him.

Two days after the heat ended, we pottered around the downstairs kitchen, making another pasta dish with cheese since that was what he craved after the heat.

"Are you sure you don't want to lie down? I'll call when I'm done."

"I'm peachy. I had a long hot shower, and it's a blizzard out there, but I'm warm. Zero complaints." Kirby gave me a crooked smile, but it wilted quickly. His cheeks were pale and his eyes red-rimmed with dark circles underneath. He was unloading the dishwasher, moving sluggishly, as if he was hungover.

I took the kitchen towel from him. "Sit down, kitten. I'll do it."

"I can't really sit right now, Hugh."

Fuck. Of course. He must be hurting. "Did you use the cream?"

"Yes."

"Painkillers?"

"Yes." Kirby put his hands on his hips, scowling at me. "Stop it. I'm okay."

"I'm sorry. Sorry." I blew out a breath. "I'll back off."

He took a step closer and patted my chest. "It's fine. I'm glad you're here."

He was touching me. Was he even aware of it? I looked at his hand on my pec and back at his face. Kirby frowned, staring at his hand thoughtfully.

"Huh. It doesn't bother me if I can control it. That's nice to know."

"Do you want to go lie down, kitten? I'll bring dinner upstairs to the living room when it's done. You can eat resting on your side."

Kirby leaned in even closer, and I stood frozen like a statue so I wouldn't spook him. He gave me the tiniest peck on the cheek. "Thank you." With that, he turned and walked out of the kitchen.

I stared at the empty doorway for a moment. His behavior toward me—it had changed. The need he used to have to distance himself every time we'd gotten closer seemed to be disappearing.

My phone dinged with the timer, announcing the pasta was done. I drained it, grated some extra cheese, and put sour cream on the tray by the plates. Cherry tomatoes, some fresh basil, salt and pepper shakers just in case—I surveyed the result. A decent dinner. I'd make us drinks at the upstairs bar.

I carried the tray to the living room and paused at the top of the stairs. Kirby stood by the bay windows, gazing at the blizzard outside. The snowflakes, illuminated by the house lights, swirled and danced, attacking the windows and flowing away.

"What are you thinking about?"

Kirby spun around. His eyes were unguarded, sad and tender. "Just remembering stuff."

I set the tray on the coffee table and joined him by the windows. "From before?"

"Yeah." He sighed. "The winter Emerson met Burke, it was snowing like this every other day for weeks. Well, you remember. And I was trying to find a place for him to stay for his first heat while he was hiding in a squat close to the docks. Except I got delayed, and when I came back, I couldn't find him. Of course, he was already safe with Burke by then, but I didn't know that. I searched for him in the blizzard for days before it occurred to me to check the pub." He shook his head, his smile self-deprecating. "I hope I'll never take it for granted. The life I have now."

To me it seemed his life was still pretty fucking difficult.

He stretched his arms above his head. "I'm hungry. What did you make?"

"Pasta carbonara. Plenty of cheese."

Kirby hurried to the table and sniffed the air above the tray. "Oh, I love you! That smells delicious!"

Did he even hear what he said? I bit my tongue.

We ate in silence, Kirby lounging on the sofa like a Roman emperor and me by his feet, sitting cross-legged on the floor.

After that, I made us drinks.

"Alcohol?" I double-checked.

"Why not. It's not like you'll get me drunk."

"No. Not today."

"Besides, you've already gotten into my pants, so no need." He smiled at his joke, but I didn't.

"You know that's not what I was after, right?"

Kirby dropped his gaze. "I know," he said quietly.

I made his favorite—Aperol spritz with fresh oranges—and settled next to him on the sofa.

"Kirby, how are you really?"

"Recovery is always shit. Emotionally and physically." He took a gulp of his drink and met my gaze. "It's not a state when I can think straight. Be sure of what I feel. You know?"

I did know. Things had changed between us, irrevocably, but Kirby needed more time.

"It's okay. Can you do one thing for me, though?"

"Sure. What?" He did trust me, thank heavens. There was zero suspicion in his tone, just automatic agreement.

"When something feels off, something I can change or help you with, tell me. Immediately."

His deep, catlike eyes studied me with curiosity. "I will."

"Thanks."

He shook his head infinitesimally, like he thought I was being weird, but then he smiled.

CHAPTER 20

KIRBY

After staring at it uselessly for days, I could finally take a walk on the beach again. Hugh wanted to come, but I said no. He seemed hurt, and I almost changed my mind looking into his puppy eyes. But I needed to think.

The wind had calmed down, murky waves had washed away most of the snow, and the wet sand had frozen solid, creating a sidewalk along the shore. Wrapped up in layers and a woolen hat, I took off north, where the beach houses were gradually smaller and farther apart. Steely clouds obscured the weak winter sun, the air freezing, but my fast pace soon warmed me up.

I didn't know what to do. No idea.

I'd always been the strong one. Heart of stone, tongue of a snake, quick fingers and fast legs, plus a strong stomach—that was how you made it in the streets of Dalton City. And I'd made it big. Fucked my way to a top-floor apartment with a walk-in closet and a uniformed doorman downstairs.

But I was still the same guy who'd washed his ass with a pet bottle above a public toilet in the park after being gangbanged in the bushes for the grand prize of fifty bucks. Main reason I'd made it this far? I knew people. I'd learned the hard way to trust my instincts and could tell if the guys who wanted to fuck me would pay what they promised or beat me up and leave. It was in their faces, clear as day.

I had Hugh clocked from the start. He was the type of alpha who'd buy a homeless rent boy dinner and then he wouldn't fuck him at all because he'd feel like he was taking advantage. A true unicorn. While I was more like the dirty raccoon you'd spook by the trash cans at night. I excelled at survival, but you wouldn't want to bring me home and pet me.

I couldn't figure out what a man like him would want with the likes of me. He behaved as if we were already together, a done deal. As if we were in love. A significant part of me must have been on board with the idea because I couldn't bear the thought of leaving him and going through the recovery alone. The other part of me, the clever Kirby who'd made sure I was still alive, was urging me to run and never look back.

I pulled the chilly air deep into my lungs as if I could cleanse my brain just by breathing. I'd known it was a stupid idea from the beginning, but I'd stuck my head into the sand—or more like between the pillows with my ass up —and fucked happily like there'd be no consequences.

What was I supposed to do now? I imagined saying goodbye to Hugh after a few more days and going back to the projects I had lined up. Fucking others and avoiding him.

My stomach clenched painfully, and bile rose in my throat.

Nope. No way.

It was like he'd branded me, changed me on the inside with his damned kindness and care and those nuzzling little kisses. Making love in the dark, under the duvet, his cum and sweat soaking me inside and out until I couldn't remember how any other man smelled or tasted...

I couldn't go back to who I'd been before. That should scare me, right? And in a way, it did. But what was the other feeling, the trembling energy in my gut, like butterflies on crack... It got stronger when I remembered that Hugh was waiting for me and that after a few more days of recovery, I could hug and kiss him again. Fuck him again.

I'd wanted Hugh for years, but that simple crush had grown into a full-blown infatuation. And more.

My phone buzzed in my pocket, and at first, I ignored it. It must have been Brian or someone like that. But then I pulled it out to look at the time and saw a missed call from Emerson. I called him back.

"Kirby! How are you?"

"Recovering, so meh."

"Oh. I'm sorry. Are you at home?"

"No. Still at the location."

"They're still filming?"

"Nah. Brian wrapped up days ago. It's just me and Hugh now. We filmed at Brian's beach house, and he's letting us stay for the recovery."

Emerson was quiet, and I realized what I'd said.

"Hugh? You're with Hugh?"

Shit. "Em, you can't tell anyone. Please. I just broke the NDA by telling you."

"I won't. I promise."

"Thanks."

"But..."

"I know, I know. Sounds insane, but Hugh auditioned for the role, and we did the film together. Brian adores him, and in a few months, everyone will find out. Yay," I enthused sarcastically.

"Wow. I would never... Just wow."

"You. Can't. Tell! Not even Burke. I'm serious."

"I won't tell anyone. Not even Burke. But you and Hugh? Are you like...together?"

I paused, trying to find the right words, which was enough for Emerson to jump to conclusions.

"I knew it! That's so amazing! He's been in love with you for the entire time, you know that, right? I'm so happy for you, Kirby."

In the classic Emerson manner, my friend didn't realize that everything had a dark side to it.

"We're not together."

"What?"

"We're not together," I repeated.

"That's bullshit. You guys belong with each other. It's obvious to everyone who ever saw you together. Even Richard asked about you two the other day. He assumed you'd been dating for months."

"We did the film together. Nothing more."

"But he's staying with you for the recovery."

"Yeah."

"And you wanted him to."

The first few days, it felt like I couldn't breathe without him, but I would never admit that out loud.

"Kirby, what the hell? Why are you so fucking stubborn? Don't you want Hugh?"

"That's not the issue."

"Then what's the issue?"

"I..." I groaned. "I don't know, okay? I don't know what

to do. It's like he's wormed his way into my head, like I'll never be able to function without him, and it's fucking terrifying. I have no idea how to do this!"

I was yelling. I'd never yelled at Emerson. Ever.

"I'm sorry, Em."

"That's okay," Emerson said soothingly. "I get it."

"You do? Because I sure don't."

"It's scary as hell to love someone."

"Love?"

"You love Hugh, and it scares you. That's okay. Everybody's afraid in the beginning. I was terrified when I realized how much I loved Burke. But it gets better, I promise."

"I don't even know how to be with someone, Em. I don't know how to be a...a couple. I've always done everything by myself."

"Even when you're with Hugh?"

I frowned, thinking. "He cooks for me. Says he likes it. We made goulash together according to a recipe Ilja sent us, and I can now chop onions like a champ since I had to do like twenty of them."

"See? That's a couply thing to do. Cooking together. Did you like it?"

"I guess. We watched movies too."

"Did you argue about what to watch?"

I snorted at the ridiculous idea. "No."

"Then you got it down, man. That's basically what couples do. Deciding what to eat, cooking, eating, deciding what to watch. Then maybe some sex. That's all there is to it, really."

I could rely on Emerson to make me laugh in the middle of a freakout. "The sex is good."

"I bet."

"Thanks, Em."

"So you are together?"

"Maybe."

"Can I say something even though it might make you angry?"

"Now I'm curious what it is. When did you get so cheeky, kid?"

"I learned from the best."

"Shoot. I'm listening."

"Could you go back? Like, say goodbye to Hugh and, um, keep filming?"

I blinked away the burning sensation in my eyes. "I'd have to, wouldn't I?"

"No. You could do something else. You're a model now too. You don't have to do porn anymore if you don't want to."

"But I'm okay with it, Em. I know you don't get it, but I like making porn, especially with a director like Brian."

"Maybe Hugh would be fine with it."

"I don't think so."

I couldn't imagine touching anyone else and then going home to Hugh. I just couldn't. It felt so wrong. Emerson was quiet, either not knowing what to say or waiting for more from me. But I had nothing.

"I'm not angry you asked, but I have to go, Em. It's freezing out here, and I should head back to the house. I'll call you when I'm back in the city. Say hi to Burke from me."

"I will. And I won't say a word about Hugh, I promise."

"Thanks. Love you, Em."

"Love you too."

I put the phone into my pocket and turned around. I'd walked quite far and couldn't even see the beach house anymore. The sky was darkening, so I hurried back.

Hugh was waiting for me downstairs. He seemed nervous and hovered awkwardly when I took off my shoes and coat.

"Are you okay? You weren't freezing?"

"I'm good. Sorry I was gone for so long. I talked to Emerson and walked and walked, and suddenly, I was halfway to Canada."

"You must be tired."

"It's okay. It was nice to get some air."

"Are you hungry? I can heat up the goulash."

"I'd love that."

"Want to eat upstairs again?"

"I think I can try sitting on a pillow and eat at the dining table like a human being."

Hugh chuckled. "Okay. Dinner like human beings. Movie later?"

"Sure."

Deciding what to eat and what to watch. Seemed we had the basics covered.

THE CONVERSATION with Emerson had done something to me. Like he'd planted a seed, and now there were things growing all over my head. Was I in love? I'd certainly never felt like this about any other person but Hugh. Could I be in a relationship? What would happen with my career? Did Hugh want the same?

I'd been distracted for the entire evening, almost jittery. The film had ended, credits rolling, but I stared at the screen, analyzing what Hugh had said and done during the past few days and what it might mean. I barely knew what we'd watched.

"Kirby?"

"Huh?"

"I asked if you wanted another drink."

"Oh. Sure. Yeah." It would be my second for the evening. Drinking too much during recovery was stupid, but Hugh knew. He wouldn't let me get drunk.

"Aperol?"

"Yes please."

He moved to the bar counter, and I shifted on the sofa, resting on my other side. Sitting was still a challenge with my sore ass, but I felt significantly better.

Could I ask Hugh what he was thinking? Maybe he wasn't interested after all, and I was just twisting myself up for nothing. Should we be having such a conversation while I was recovering? But I felt quite sane. Well, aside from the fact that I was contemplating being in love, I was sane.

"What's going on, kitten? You're miles away."

"Sorry. Um. Things on my mind."

"What things?"

Hugh flashed me a curious look before refocusing on the orange he was cutting.

Screw it. I'd never been a patient person.

"You," I said.

"Shit!" He hissed, startling me. The knife clattered to the bar counter and down onto the floor. Hugh hurried to the sink and shoved his hand under a stream of water.

"Oh no. I'm sorry." I shot up off the sofa and ran around the counter to join him.

Hugh held his left pointer finger under the stream.

"How deep is it? Let me see."

A thin cut ran over the first knuckle. I was relieved to see it wasn't serious. "That doesn't need stitches, but I bet it stings like hell."

"It's fine. Just startled me."

"I'm sorry."

"What are *you* sorry for? It was me who cut my finger."

"Yeah, but I said..."

Holding Hugh's hand in both of mine, I looked up. He was gazing at me with a patient smile on his beautiful face, his eyes warm. Loving.

"You've been thinking about me for the whole day?"

I could feel color rising into my cheeks. "Yes."

"And? Have you come to any conclusion?"

"I think I might be in love with you."

Hugh bit his lip, looking like he was suppressing a grin.

"No need to look so smug about it, man."

He laughed. "I love you, Kirby."

He just said it, like it was nothing. Smiling, even.

I gaped up at him. "You do?"

"You're my omega. My mate. And I love you."

"Mate?"

"Yes. We're mates."

"But..."

I couldn't look away from his glowing expression. He seemed so happy. So sure.

"We'll figure it out, kitten, don't worry. Now come help me wrap this up so I don't bleed all over you, okay?"

"Oh."

True enough, I had blood smears on my hands.

We went to the bathroom, and I taped up Hugh's finger with a Band-Aid. Then he finished making the drinks and gestured for me to follow him. At the end of the hallway was a big sunroom with a hot tub, which was now illuminated with dim spotlights.

"You turned on the tub?"

"This morning. The water should be warm enough

now. Brian messaged to knock ourselves out, and I figured you might be well enough to do this today." Hugh clicked some switch, and the water started bubbling away. I couldn't wait to soak in there.

"This looks amazing."

We stripped and lowered ourselves into the tub. I sipped the drink, realizing it was weak. He must have used the non-alcoholic bubbly I'd seen in the fridge. Hugh was always so responsible. It made me smile.

"What are you grinning at?"

"You look like a bad boy with those tats and shaved head, but you're such a do-gooder."

"Does it bother you?"

"No. I like it."

"Then we're good."

"We are." I swallowed. "I think we are. Right?"

"Yeah."

Hugh reached out with his uninjured hand, and I gripped his fingers. I usually hated any kind of touch during recovery, but Hugh appeared to be my exception. As long as I was in control and touching him only with my fingers, I didn't mind at all. *Because he's my mate.*

"We'll figure it out?" I asked.

"From now on, it'll be easy, I promise."

He was maddeningly cheerful, damn him, but I couldn't keep circling around the hot topic. I needed to get it all out. "What about my job?"

"What do you want? Like, what would be the ideal scenario?"

"Ideal? I don't have to give a shit about reality?"

"Exactly."

"I continue making porn because that's what I'm good

at, and I keep fucking you because you're the best I've ever had."

Hugh took a sip of his drink and winked at me over the edge of the glass.

"Then let's do both," he said. "Let's keep making porn together."

I chuckled, shaking my head, but Hugh just observed me quietly, his expression serious. Was he crazy?

"You mean it?"

He shrugged. "Kirby, I love you. I want to be with you." There he went again, saying it like it was normal. As if we were talking about what to eat and which movie to watch. Love was difficult, painful, and infuriating. Wasn't it? But Hugh kept smiling. "I honestly don't care all that much about the filming, except that it tickles my exhibitionist side and pays well. I'm down for doing more stuff with Brian. Maybe not heat, because I didn't like how vulnerable you were in front of the cameras and I got overprotective. But just sex...why not? What we did on Tuesday before the heat, the trial run, that was great. I'd do it again in a heartbeat."

My head was spinning, which could have been the hot tub or the Aperol, but most probably, it was all Hugh, surprising me yet again.

"But the important thing is," he continued, "we're together now. You and me. I'm in this for real, Kirby."

I blinked, forcing the nastiest question out there. Because it had to be said. "And what if I have to fuck someone else at work?"

Hugh didn't even flinch. "Because you think you have to? No. I wouldn't like that and would try to convince you to quit. But I've had a lot of time to think about this, you know. You've had this job ever since I've known you, and

I've always wanted you anyway. I don't need you to change for me, Kirby. I only want you to be happy and love me back."

I took a gulp of my drink and sank lower into the warm water. The bubbles swirled, and the dark, cold ocean hummed outside. I closed my eyes, gathering the courage to tell him the truth.

"I don't want anyone else to touch me ever again. Only you."

As I was saying it, some sort of energy poured through our fingers, like another level of communication between us. And I knew, just like him, that we'd figure it out.

We'd be okay.

After a few beats of quiet, Hugh's deep voice wrapped itself around my heart. "Kitten, that makes me so happy. It means you're mine. You do love me, don't you?"

I squeezed his fingers because yes, I loved him. I just couldn't reply around the lump in my throat.

It had been six days and seven nights since my last heat wave. I woke up early in the morning, the bedroom still dark, and went to pee. Hugh didn't move from his position, sprawled over the bed, snoring loudly. Luckily, he only did that when he slept on his back. Feeling cold after my trip to the bathroom, I snuggled up to him under the covers and nuzzled his shoulder. He smelled so nice. Without the haze and lust of heat, his scent calmed me and made me feel safe.

And then I realized what was going on. The recovery was over. I could cuddle my alpha without cringing or feeling nauseous. Smiling, I threw my leg over his and hugged his broad chest.

Hugh hummed, sneaking an arm around my back and tugging me even closer. Mmm, he was warm, his skin against mine like the best comfort blanket.

"I love you," I said, trying the words out. It didn't feel strange or cheesy like I'd thought it would. In fact, it felt entirely right.

The mattress shifted, Hugh grunted, and suddenly I was pinned under him, with his arms framing my head and his nose brushing mine.

"You're mine," he rasped, his voice rough with sleep.

I nodded eagerly. His hard cock was pressed against my inner thigh. *Oh yes.*

"Then fuck me," I said.

With a growl, Hugh attacked my mouth.

Forget lazy, sleepy morning sex. He manhandled me until I was on my stomach with one arm twisted behind my back, then he spread my legs with his knee. He quickly checked I was wet enough, brushing his finger over my hole, and pressed his thick cockhead into me.

"Fuck, you're tight, kitten. It doesn't hurt?"

Fully healed after the heat, my hole was fighting back against the intrusion, squeezing around Hugh. Deeper in my belly, I felt empty. "Need it. Keep going."

"I guess this means you're recovered, hm?"

"Uh-huh."

He thrust, forcing his way in, and I cried out with the stretch and pressure. "This what you want?"

"Yes!"

I wanted him to claim me, and he must have sensed what I needed because he took me roughly and fast, pounding my hole until our skin slapped together. My climax ripped through me, making me wail and twitch, and I thought I heard Hugh laugh between the wild groans and growling noises he was making. He shoved his big cock deep enough to make me yelp from the sudden pressure in my guts, and he bit my shoulder. Hard. Oh, the sting was delicious. It made me come again, just a little one, like a powerful aftershock. He lay on top of me, panting, his weight pinning me into the mattress, and I was grinning like a fool.

Seemed like I got myself a man. A gorgeous, sexy hunk of an alpha, with a magical dick and a growly whiskey voice. All mine. As his cum seeped into my hole, I closed my eyes and thought of how he'd taken care of me during the past week. How patient he'd been and considerate, and how he made me feel wanted and important even when he couldn't come near me. The recovery had been mild, the easiest I'd had, even though the heat had been the most powerful. Was it always like that when you were with the right person?

"Can I stay inside you a bit longer?" Hugh shifted, his cock still half hard.

"Yes. Feels great."

"I've missed you," he murmured, peppering kisses all over my shoulders and neck. "Missed kissing you, fucking you. Missed your taste."

"Missed your cock."

He chuckled and thrust deliberately, sending a frisson of fresh arousal through my insides.

He didn't soften entirely. He rocked us gently, and after a little while, he grew fully hard again.

"Someone's keen today," I teased.

"I've been staring at that pert ass of yours for a week. I'm far from done with you."

"Want to give me one more load before breakfast?"

Abruptly, he was gone, and I cried out with the sudden emptiness.

"Hey!"

But he gripped my ankles and dragged me across the bed until I was on my back, my ass hanging off the mattress. He folded my legs to my chest and appraised my hole. I felt the cum leak out, and Hugh groaned. He scooped it up with his fingers and shoved it back into me. Then he pressed his cockhead against my sloppy opening.

"You're a mess already."

"I love it. Mess me up until I'm sore and covered with cum and slick."

"Naughty kitty." A devious grin stretched his lips as he inched into me. He roamed my body with his burning gaze.

"Going to do you slow now. Want to watch you lose it."

"Won't take long." I sucked in a harsh breath when his cockhead dragged over my gland. Then it touched the mouth to my womb, reminding me of all those epic breeding orgasms, and my eyes rolled back into my head.

If this was the sex I was going to have for the rest of my life, I'd die happy.

CHAPTER 21

HUGH

During breakfast, Kirby seemed a little unsure again. I kept touching him—kissing his forehead, stroking his neck, brushing his arms—not just because I wanted to reassure him, but because I couldn't help myself. Now that he had recovered and accepted my closeness, I couldn't get enough of him.

He was jittery but smiling, insecurity and excitement battling in his features. When my phone dinged on the table, he jumped, almost spilling his coffee into his eggs.

"Sorry. That's just Jay." I read the message and put the phone aside. I'd reply later.

"Oh!" Kirby's eyes went wide. "It's Christmas Day today, isn't it?"

"Well, yeah."

"You're supposed to be with them now." His face showed it all, like an open book: regret, fear, guilt. My Kirby. He didn't want to part from me, just like I couldn't bear the thought of being away from him—not yet. But he felt guilty for keeping me away from my family.

"It's okay." Something occurred to me, and I wondered if it would be too soon, but I couldn't resist trying. "You could come with me, you know. If you want."

"To your place? That's...early?" He studied his eggs as if the answer was written in the yolks.

"They already know you. Jay likes you."

"You know I'm shit with kids."

"I think you're underestimating yourself. But anyway, you don't have to interact with Monty more than saying hi, you know. He'll be occupied with his presents."

Kirby stiffened, staring at me in horror. "Presents? I can't go. I have nothing."

"Kirby. Chill. Main question. Do you want to go?"

He blinked. "I have to buy presents, Hugh. I can't barge into your home on Christmas morning and bring nothing."

"They don't expect anything."

But Kirby was already typing away on his phone. "The big mall off ninety-nine is open. Some stores have reduced hours, though. We can stop by there, and maybe we'll get lucky?"

"I'm glad you're coming with me, Kirby."

He blinked as if he'd just realized he'd practically said yes already. "Sure. Um. What should we buy? What does Monty like?"

"We'll see what we can find. He's into dinosaurs, of course. And Lego."

"Huh. You'll have to help me choose."

"They'll be happy we're coming."

After we finished breakfast and cleaned up the kitchen, Kirby went to pack and I called Jay.

"Merry Christmas, big brother."

"Merry Christmas, Jaybird. Listen, would it be okay if I brought Kirby over today? I know it's a bit sudden, but I don't want to leave him alone on Christmas Day, and honestly, we're kinda attached at the hip now after the heat. I don't want to let him out of my sight."

"You're together? For real?"

"I think so."

Jay screeched, and I had to hold the phone farther away from my ear.

"I take it you're fine with us coming over?"

"Of course! I'm so happy for you. And Monty will be over the moon Uncle Hugh's coming after all. When can you be here?"

"I have to check with Kirby. We need to pack our stuff and take a cab. Maybe three hours?"

"Great. Text me when you're on the way."

"Love you, Jay. Thanks."

"This is amazing, Hugh. You're happy, right?"

"I am. Very."

Jay sighed contentedly, the phone crackling. "I'd better check on the turkey then. See you!"

"See you soon."

The packing was fast. We hadn't brought much since we knew we'd spend the two weeks naked most of the time. Finding a cab was next to impossible, though. I was calling a third service, getting no response, when Kirby poured a set of car keys into my hand.

"One of Brian's. He says Merry Christmas and to bring it to the studio after the holidays. It's in the garage."

I blinked. *Rich people.* "Okay. You don't want to drive?"

Kirby threw me a look as if I were stupid. "I don't have a license, Hughie. C'mon."

We did find a Lego set with dinosaurs in one of the few open stores at the mall. I thought it was way too expensive, but Kirby couldn't be swayed. He also insisted on buying Jay a set of silk pajamas, claiming I wouldn't get it since I was an alpha, but that Jay would love it. He sat in the passenger seat with the shopping bag on his lap, fidgeting nervously for the entire drive to our place.

Finding a parking place wasn't easy, but we managed to grab a spot a couple of blocks away. It was freezing again, the first few snowflakes swirling in the air, signaling another heavy snowfall for the night. The winters in Dalton City were truly evil sometimes.

"You ready?" I asked, the keys to my apartment in my hand.

Kirby blew out a breath and nodded.

As soon as I inserted the key into the lock, stomps came from the hallway inside. Monty tore the door open and hugged me.

"Hugh! Dad said you wouldn't be back for Christmas."

"I didn't think I would make it, but it worked out in the end."

"Do you have more presents?"

"I already left you a few under the tree with the ones from Santa."

Monty cocked his head. "Santa doesn't exist."

Kirby snickered next to me.

"Who's that?"

"That's Kirby, remember? You've met him at the pub. Say hi."

"Hiii," Monty drew out, studying Kirby suspiciously. "Why are you here?"

Kirby stiffened. "Um—"

"Be nice," I said, pointing at my nephew. "I invited

Kirby because I like him and wanted him to be with us on Christmas."

"I...got presents," Kirby said in a shaky voice. His nervousness was adorable.

Jay appeared with a kitchen towel over his shoulder and went straight after Kirby. He hugged him, which made Kirby freeze at first, but then he gingerly returned the hug. "I'm so glad you could come. The turkey is not nearly done, sorry, but I got soup and salad and shortbread."

"Hi. Thanks for having me," Kirby stammered out when Jay let him breathe.

"Kirby says he has presents for us," Monty announced.

Jay grimaced at Kirby and mouthed, "sorry," but Kirby just smiled.

"You can't badger guests about presents. That's rude," I said, and the little shit groaned like a teen.

After hanging up our damp coats, we settled in the living room with tea and shortbread. Monty showed off the action figures from me and the race car models that Burke and Emerson got him. He seemed happy with his loot. When he unwrapped the Lego set from Kirby, his eyes got so big they almost fell out. He jumped up and threw himself at Kirby, squeezing his neck. Kirby looked horrified by the sudden display of affection, but luckily, Monty was too hyped up to molest him much longer. He ran to the kitchen where Jay was checking on the food.

"Dad! Dad! Kirby got me the big box Lenny has. You said it was too expensive, but Kirby got it for me."

Jay appeared in the living room.

"Oh wow. You didn't have to do that."

Kirby shrugged, blushing furiously.

"Do you want to build it with me?" Monty asked him.

"Um. I don't know how to do that. I've never done it before."

Jay gave him a sappy, compassionate look, which Kirby didn't notice, thank fuck.

"What? That's crazy," Monty said. "Everyone can build Legos. C'mon, I'll show you. It's super simple. You got pictures, and you have to be careful so the pages don't stick together because then it doesn't fit in the end, and you have to redo it all."

Seeming a little lost but not unhappy, Kirby sat with Monty on the carpet and looked for the right bricks while Monty put them together.

Jay unwrapped his own present, his eyes doing the same thing as Monty's. He looked at me all shocked, mouthing something unintelligible, and I shrugged. Yes, my boyfriend was well off, so he brought stuff we'd never dare to buy ourselves.

When the turkey was almost ready, I went to the kitchen to help Jay set the table, leaving Kirby engrossed in the Lego set. He was cute as hell.

My little brother cornered me by the stove, his hands on his hips and a shit-eating grin on his face.

"I think this time it's for keeps," I whispered.

Jay squealed and tackle-hugged me.

"You weren't particularly shit with Monty," I told Kirby once we were cuddled up in my bed. It had taken ages to calm Monty down after all the hype, and when he'd finally fallen asleep, we'd been groggy. Jay excused himself to go to bed, and Kirby and I holed ourselves up in my room.

"Older kids aren't as scary as babies."

I chuckled. "Babies are scary?"

"Yeah. Like you never know if they're fine or if you're doing something stupid to them because they can't tell you. They keep crying even when there's nothing wrong with them. I mean, they can be sick and dying, or their socks are itchy. I have no idea how Emerson deals with that."

I bit my tongue to keep myself from laughing since Kirby sounded dead serious.

"Well, Monty had a wonderful time with you, so thank you."

"He's cool," Kirby said noncommittally. "Glad he liked the Lego."

"You've made his year. He isn't used to getting such expensive toys."

"Shit. Do you think Jay's mad at me because of that?"

"No. Of course not. He's excited about us, in fact."

"Yeah?"

"Uh-huh. He's happy that I finally caught the man of my dreams."

"Caught, huh? So I'm prey, big man?"

"You've been evading me for three years, but now you're finally mine." I bit his ear lightly, and he giggled, squirming.

Humming, I nosed behind his ear and down his neck, pulling in his scent. How happy could one man be?

Abruptly, Kirby turned in my arms and kissed me lightly on the lips. He had his thoughtful frown on. "Jay needs a lot of help with Monty, so you can't stay at my place all the time. And that's fine, I totally get it. But do you think he'd be okay with me staying over every once in a while?"

I'd thought about that a lot. It would be a challenge to fit enough time into my schedule to include Kirby as much as I wanted to, especially since I'd prefer having him by my side twenty-four seven. But it was early days, and something told me we wouldn't have to juggle our schedules for long.

"I'm sure it'll be okay. And on weekends, when I don't have to bring Monty to school, I'll stay with you, and we could meet them in the afternoons." I studied his reaction to the proposed family time carefully. Monty was my kid too, for all intents and purposes. Did Kirby realize that?

I needn't have worried. Kirby gifted me with one of his rare shy smiles. "I'd like that."

I kissed his nose, and he snuggled up against me with a soft sigh. Smelling him and having him in my bed made me hard. My body hadn't yet gotten used to the fact that I could touch and kiss my omega whenever I wanted, and my cock was constantly overexcited. Kirby snuck his hand between us, caressing my erection through my pajamas.

"And what would Jay think if we had sex in here?"

"We're adults. As long as we're quiet—"

The rest of my sentence got cut off when Kirby shoved his tongue into my mouth.

We made love slowly and quietly, hidden under the covers. I fucked him deep, facing him, taking in his beautiful face as he struggled not to cry out. He came with a muted moan, his head tucked to my chest.

I used my briefs to wipe us off and spooned my omega on the bed. He smelled like raw sex, a little like me, and a lot like honey and coconut.

"Maybe one day, we could live together," I whispered, but Kirby didn't reply. He must have been asleep already.

Smiling, I imagined a future where Jay had found someone decent and lived close to us. I would still see Monty several times a week, we'd do trips to the park on Sundays and eat dinner together. In that future, I didn't have to compromise anything. My Kirby would sleep in my arms every night, and my family would be happy and safe.

CHAPTER 22

KIRBY

The first Friday in January, Hugh and I sat once more in front of the camera, except this time, we were clothed. Mostly. The stylist chose only jeans for Hugh—I caught the sneaky fucker drooling over my man's magnificent chest. The pants I wore were seriously one of the most beautiful pieces of clothing I'd ever gotten my paws on, and the stylist told me I could keep them after the shoot, so I wasn't all that mad about him acting a little inappropriate. Soon, the whole country would be having wet dreams about Hugh Urban, and as long as no one hit on him right in front of me, I was pretty sure I'd enjoy the boyfriend envy.

The thin, shimmering fabric of the pants felt like a breeze on my skin, and even Hugh must have liked them because he kept rubbing my thigh. Brian had us positioned on a big fluffy bed against a mountain of pillows. I didn't know the cameraman, but since we weren't going to do anything but talk, I didn't care.

"As you know," Brian told me while the crew was

setting up, "Hugh promised me this interview in exchange for leaving you alone the last three days of the heat. I'm going to use a few clips as promotional material on the website and social media. The full interview will be added as a bonus to the director's cut."

"I'm not answering anything private," I said.

Brian flashed me an annoyed glare. "You're already showing your privates."

That comment made me bristle. "Really, Brian? You went there with me? It's different, and you know it. Showing my body is one thing, exposing my personal life is another level entirely."

Taking a deep breath, Brian rubbed his hands together. This time, the gesture seemed tense. "I apologize, Kirby, for my thoughtless remark. I promise I'm not going to ask you anything that would compromise your personal integrity. It's meant to be quite wholesome."

Hugh patted my leg. "If we think a question is outside our comfort zone, we'll just stay quiet. Is that okay?"

"Sure," Brian muttered. I was still pissed at him. It wasn't like him to say that kind of shit. Was he nervous about the interview? He seemed to think that saying how we got together during the filming would go viral and blow up the movie's popularity, but I wasn't convinced. People wanted scandals and not boring happy couples.

"Ready," the technician said.

Brian clapped in front of the main camera.

"Have you seen the film already?" he asked as if he didn't know.

"Only snippets of it," Hugh answered. He cast his arm around my shoulders and rested his left hand on my leg. I liked it when he showed his ownership of me. No, scratch that, I loved his possessiveness, especially in public.

"Did you watch it together?"

"Yeah."

"What did you think?"

Hugh looked at me, smirking. "At first, we didn't do much thinking at all."

I bit my lip to keep myself from laughing. In truth, after Brian had shown us a few clips, we'd hidden in the studio bathrooms, and I'd sucked Hugh off. With the visuals from my heat fresh in my mind, I'd come in my pants from the taste of his cum alone.

"Hugh, you're a relative beginner. Did you find it arousing to see yourself like that?"

I had to admit that so far, the questions were benign.

"Um. Not seeing myself, no. But it was intoxicating to see *us* together. To see Kirby lost in pleasure because of what I was doing to him. That was incredible."

"Kirby?"

"I like this job. I get off on it. But this was different."

"How different?"

"The sex felt different, and from the scenes I've seen, I think it shows."

"Because...?" Brian prompted, raising his eyebrows. I wasn't excited about announcing my feelings like that, but at the same time, I didn't see anything wrong with it either.

"I was falling in love with Hugh."

Hugh kissed my temple, tightening his hold on me. Brian beamed at me like I'd made his year, and I had to look down to hide the grimace his cheesy enthusiasm brought on.

"Hugh, how did you feel during the filming?"

"Angry and frustrated."

"Can you elaborate?"

"I had trouble controlling my instincts. Kirby was

vulnerable, and I felt protective of him. My alpha decided that Kirby was my mate, and I hoped he returned my feelings, but I couldn't be sure. I had to remind myself often that I was, in fact, working. More often than not, I got lost in Kirby and forgot about the cameras."

"What was the most difficult part?"

I glared at Brian, but he just smiled innocently.

Hugh sighed, looking down, so I gripped his hand in both of mine.

"Two things. Not being able to change the past and not knowing whether I'd be allowed to touch Kirby again after the filming was over."

"What do you mean by changing the past?"

"I can only be honest about my own feelings," he hedged.

I turned to face him. "I think what Hugh means is that he was angry about what had happened to me before I met him. Folks who follow me know about me being homeless before doing porn. My first three heats were spent with people who treated me like shit. I recovered on the street and in shelters."

Hugh kept his eyes on our joined hands, not saying anything.

"You can cut this out," I told Brian. "I don't want to be a downer."

"I decide," Brian said, looking all smug. "We wrapped up the filming on the sixth day of your heat. Can you tell me a little about the last three days you spent together alone?"

"We did it under the covers," I said, grinning at the camera, and Brian laughed.

"I'm exhibitionist enough to find it arousing that people will see us having sex," Hugh said. "But that's just a kink. A hot little detail that we both like sometimes. Being together just us for the rest of the heat and Kirby's recovery allowed us to connect in a way we wouldn't have been able to do while working. I could focus on Kirby alone and take care of him how I needed."

Hugh's easy honesty was making me squirm. My big alpha man was better at expressing feelings than I'd ever be.

"Kirby, how was your recovery?"

"Physically easier than ever before. I was just confused."

"Why?"

"It's never happened to me before that I was so...hung up on a coworker on set. I was afraid of the consequences it would have for my career and my private life. Hugh stayed by my side, though, letting me figure it out in peace. He was incredibly patient with me."

"Are you a couple now?"

"Yes," I said decisively, and Hugh lifted his gaze to mine, smiling happily. "As Hugh said, we're mates."

"Does it mean that Kirby Matthews is quitting porn?"

"I won't be doing any heat stuff. I know you shouldn't say never. But after Hugh and I have gotten a few days by ourselves thanks to the generosity of our director"—I winked at Brian—"I'm pretty sure I want to spend my heats with him in private from now on."

"That's heats, though. What about other genres? Are you quitting or not?"

"I won't be filming with other people. Whether we do something together is up to my man to decide."

"Hugh?"

Hugh searched my gaze for a long time, and the fire in

his eyes crackled. His lips twitched with a suppressed smile.

"We'll see."

I took that as a resounding yes.

THAT SATURDAY, we were having a movie night with Monty because Jay went out on a blind date a colleague of his had arranged. Hugh joked around with his nephew playing games, then he put on the newest superhero flick. I could hover on the fringes and stuff my face with nachos and popcorn. We barely managed to send Monty to bed before Jay came home.

"How did it go?" I asked. I could see in Jay's face that his evening hadn't been a total catastrophe, but was it normal to be home this early? I'd never been on a proper first date, so what did I know?

"He was charming, asking a bunch of follow-up questions, all engrossed and fascinated that I was a nurse and single father and how hard I must have worked and blah blah blah. I'm suspicious."

"Not possible he's just a good guy?" Hugh quipped from where he was putting away the dishes.

"Not with the way he looks. Too perfect."

"I'm with Jay on this one," I said. "Good-looking nice guys are usually creepy."

Hugh threw the kitchen towel onto the counter and put his hands on his hips, glowering at Jay and me. "What am I then?"

"You're a porn-making, spanking, tattooed bad boy, lover. Not a nice guy in sight."

Jay laughed. "Kirby's right, Hugh. You're too edgy."

"But I am nice," Hugh protested.

I stood, putting my arm around his waist. "Yes, you are. Honestly, you're a fucking saint. But shh. Nobody can know, or our reputation is ruined."

Snickering, Jay waved us off. "Go home. I can't deal with you two tonight. I'm exhausted."

"We're going." Hugh gripped my neck and pushed me toward the hallway. I happily let him. I had a surprise for him, and since we could sleep in on Sunday, I was going to try it on as soon as we got home.

"Skate park tomorrow," Jay reminded us. "Monty is looking forward to showing off his new tricks."

"Yes. We'll be there at two."

"And thanks for tonight." Jay hugged me in the hallway, and I managed not to squirm. I would eventually get used to this family stuff. Hopefully.

Twenty minutes later, Hugh kissed me, lifting me up against the elevator wall. I had to resolutely push him away when we entered the apartment, or we'd end up doing it on the floor by the door. Then he wanted to shower together but begrudgingly agreed when I told him to go first.

"Trust me," I said, and he relented, planting one last kiss on my cheek before disappearing into the bathroom.

He waited in bed while I took my turn.

Showered and with my teeth brushed, I eyed my newest outfit. Lace and silk, my favorite materials, the colors ranging from soft pink to peach and gold. I loved the contrast between the intricate flowery patterns in innocent hues and the obscene cut of the lingerie. The shorts were high, almost to my belly button, but open in the back, exposing my crease. In the front, they hugged my cock and balls, the fabric transparent, with a fly for easy access. I could leave them on when we fucked. The top was only long lace sleeves connected to a high collar. My nipples were exposed. I brushed my fingers over them, pinching the tips. Then I carefully attached the small golden clamps connected by a chain. The jewel looked gorgeous on my exposed chest framed by the lace. When I walked to the bathroom door, my nipples ached, and I grew hard from anticipation alone.

I stepped into the bedroom with my heart beating double-time.

Hugh sat up, his phone falling from his hands and mouth hanging open.

"Oh my God."

Slowly, I turned, showing off the assless shorts.

"Fucking hell, kitten. Stay there."

I obeyed. Brushing my fingers along the edges of the lace over my ass cheeks, I let my alpha look his fill.

"You're stunning, love. Breathtaking," he rasped, and I bit my lip. He was aroused. A lot, by the sound of his voice. Normally, I didn't splurge money on luxury stuff—except for underwear. And this had been an investment well made.

He walked over to me and knelt behind me. Running his hands up my legs, he nuzzled my ass cheeks and trailed kisses along the edges of the lace. He gently tugged on the chain connecting the nipple clamps, and I gasped.

"Spread your legs."

Wanting to give him better access, I braced my hands on the closet door and pushed my hips out. Hugh groaned. The first swipe of his tongue over my hole made me shiver.

Rimming me deep, he played with the lace and the chain, and I trembled, trying to stay upright.

"I'm close, Hugh."

"I know." He licked up my crease a few times and patted my ass.

"Get on the bed. On your knees."

I knelt on the edge of the mattress. On my elbows and knees, I arched my back, pushing my ass up. I swayed my hips, taunting my alpha. Hugh just stood there and watched, stroking his thick erection.

"You look almost too pretty for what I want to do to you."

"What do you want to do to me?"

"I want to spank your rosy ass while you keep those panties on. And then I want to fuck you in them until they're soaked with your cum and slick."

"Please, Hugh."

The spanks were gentle, only warming stings, just how I liked it. I wasn't into pain, but a spanking from Hugh never got painful and never felt like a punishment or power play. It relaxed me, sensitized my skin, and made my hole wet. He worked my ass over from different angles, humming when he appraised me.

"All pink and pretty. So gorgeous. Push with your ass, kitty."

I did as I was told, pushing out slick.

"Good omega," Hugh praised.

And then his cock was in me.

I cried out with surprise when he filled me to the root in a single thrust. Without pause, he pulled out and roughly slammed back in. My inner muscles fluttered around him, and my erection throbbed, the lace suddenly tight. The gentle scratch felt glorious on my leaking cock.

Hugh sped up, holding me by my hips. The chain connecting the clamps swayed with the thrusts, pulling on my nipples, and when Hugh's thick cockhead punched the mouth to my womb, I lost it.

He knew how I liked it. Fast, hard, and deep, root to tip, he plowed me with his fat dick until my hole squelched, all loose and full of slick.

I came three times at least. When I was all but drooling into the pillow, mewling, Hugh slowed down, circling his hips. His cock jerked inside me.

"You look like a blushing virgin in those panties. You're so wet, horny boy. All spanked and fucked out. I'll soak your pretty hole with cum."

I smiled because his crude words meant he was close and lost in the act.

"Fuck, yes. Gorgeous hole. Suck my dick with your ass. Mmm."

But then he pulled out.

Before I could protest, I was on my back with a pillow under my butt. Hugh sank inside me and kissed me.

And then he dragged the duvet over us.

"Want to come like this," he murmured against my lips.

He fucked me slowly but deeply, kissing me in the dark, and I melted. A lazy climax built in my core, spilling into my stomach and legs, and when my hole began clenching again, Hugh groaned.

His cum filled me as I came one last time, completely liquefied.

"I love you, love you." It felt so easy saying it now. I recalled the first time we'd made love like this, hidden from the world, and the surge of happiness almost brought tears to my eyes. "I love you so much, Hugh. Come in me. I love you."

Caught in a long orgasm, Hugh didn't reply. He grunted and gasped for breath, his hips stuttering. I deliberately tightened my inner muscles, milking his cock, and he cried out wildly. Then he buried himself in me as deep as he could and stilled.

"Fuck, Kirby. You feel... *Fuck*." He gave out a loud, almost painful groan and rocked his hips one more time. "My omega. All mine."

I was. All of me.

A shudder ran through him, and he exhaled, slumping over me. "I love you so much."

I adored the sense of rightness and contentment Hugh brought me whenever we held each other like this. As if he protected me, filling me up where I felt empty, in my body and my heart, and shielding me where I was exposed. Like we were two parts of the same thing that only made sense when we were together.

"Do you like the outfit then?" I asked innocently once we were both breathing normally again. "I can't return it now since the panties are full of my cum."

Hugh laughed, shaking us both.

"You look like a sexy, wicked angel. Nobody will ever see you like this but me, okay? Promise." He brushed his hand over my chest, gently removing the clamps and massaging my nipples.

"I promise. I'll only ever wear it for you."

"My naughty little kitten."

"Now I have to get the cum off the shorts, though."

"I don't mind washing them for you."

"You're kinky in the weirdest ways."

Hugh lifted his head and looked at me, all sheepish. "I still have the yellow ones from our first night together. I put them in my pocket and forgot about them. Then I found them when I came home. They're in my nightstand."

My eyes grew big. "You stole my yellow briefs?"

"Unintentionally at first. But...I might have kept them intentionally."

I grinned, tapping my lips with a fingertip. "Good to know." Tonight wasn't the last time I would dress up in lace for my alpha.

EPILOGUE

HUGH

One month later

I'd be eternally grateful to Brian for letting us watch the final cut of the movie alone. I was so tense. I felt a little sick to my stomach, but our director had been lyrical about the result, claiming it would be another hit. That meant it couldn't be too bad, right?

Holding my hand, Kirby sat next to me, fidgeting like he always did when he was nervous. The start confused me because I hadn't even noticed they'd filmed us like that. The clip showed Kirby standing in a bathrobe next to me, leaning his head on my shoulder in front of the living room bay windows. It was snowing outside. Then the focus shifted to Kirby's face as he gazed up at me. His face shone with obvious affection. It was strange watching him looking at me, like I was peeping in on my own life, but at the same time, the unique perspective gave me a deep sense of rightness. We looked like we belonged with each other, already in the first minute of the film.

I felt Kirby squirm next to me, sucking in a breath here and there as the film continued. My mouth on his nipples, on his wet ass, my hands squeezing his flesh, my wet cock sinking into his heated hole, his eyes rolling back into his head, ropes of cum on his chest, my nostrils flaring and teeth bared when I came inside him... Kirby's underbelly bulged with my knot, his reddened cock twitching with a breeding orgasm, and I shook, my hips snapping forward erratically. My moans sounded like I was in pain, and Kirby slid his hand over his stomach and breathed a long drawn-out yesss of approval... A single drop of cum bubbled up from where we were joined, squeezed out from around the knot as if Kirby's insides were overflowing with it. I wouldn't have thought it was possible to see someone being bred so obviously and explicitly, but then the camera traveled up Kirby's body, over his distorted belly, his aroused nipples, then it lingered on his smiling lips...

Fuck.

Suddenly, Kirby was on me, undoing my fly and pulling out my cock. After hastily dropping his pants and under-wear, he took me into his hole with his back to my chest and rolled his hips, moaning loudly.

And that was how we watched the breeding scene by the bay windows, with him riding my cock. Our bodies tangled on the screen, our cries and moans cresting through the speakers, we fucked as we watched ourselves fuck, and my blood was boiling in my veins.

Close in no time, I grabbed Kirby's cock and milked it. He bore down, coming hard, his seed spilling over my fist. The clenching heat of his body brought on my own climax, and I bucked up into him, coating his insides with my cum. Kirby slumped, breathing harshly.

The other Kirby, the one on the screen, keened with another breeding orgasm, and the close-up showed his hole, his drawn-up balls, and how his taint swelled with my knot growing inside him.

"Fuck, kitty, we're hot."

"Uh-huh. Don't move. I can't watch this without your dick in me."

"I could stay hard for a week, seeing you like that."

The next clip blew my mind. Brian left my furious face in the movie. In the scene, I sat on the floor with Kirby in my lap, holding him protectively while glaring daggers at the camera. It looked so primal, so very alpha; I understood why he put it in.

"I don't remember this," Kirby said.

"You were out of it, locked in breeding with me. Cameron almost stepped on your hand, and I lost my shit, demanding they stop filming. Brian was fuming."

"Wow. But it couldn't have been too bad if he left it in."

"I imagine not."

"You look hot when you're angry. I wonder—"

And next scene.

We were in the shower, kissing and caressing each other, all biting lips and hungry gazes, and I could feel the longing reverberate through me.

"I wanted to keep you forever. Craved you so much, I was driving myself crazy," I whispered into Kirby's ear, my eyes on the screen.

Kirby hummed and wiggled, deliberately clamping on my still-hard cock lodged inside him.

We moved slowly, gently fucking while watching the rest. And I had to admit to being impressed with the result.

It was filth, complete and utter filth, that kept me hard inside Kirby for a solid hour and a half. But with the clever cuts and brilliantly captured play of emotion, Brian had told the story of us falling in love during Kirby's heat, and it was striking.

After seeing Kirby's face in some of the scenes, whether with his devoted gaze pinned on me or with his eyes closed, his lips curved in a blissful smile, I *knew* he loved me. It was all in there, in every touch we shared, every kiss, every rough thrust and careful caress. Brian, the fucking genius he was, had pulled off the impossible—he'd managed to make a porno about love.

The credits rolled, and Kirby lifted and sank down onto my cock with a moan. By that point, my jeans were drenched with his slick, and I was aching for another release.

I flipped him, throwing him onto the sofa and slapping his ass.

"On your knees, chest down, ass up."

He scrambled to obey and held his ass cheeks spread for me. His relaxed hole gaped open.

I took him how he liked it, hard and fast, and he groaned happily into the sofa cushions.

"Yeah. Like that. Use my hole."

He came before I did, keening and mumbling he loved me. I fucked him for a while longer, using his softened body like he'd asked me to, before I let myself succumb to pleasure, holding my omega by his hips as I poured my cum into him.

"Well, that was fun," Kirby said breezily, still bent over with his ass on display. I kissed it and brushed my thumb over the sloppy opening. Kirby clenched and relaxed his hole, and a dollop of cum escaped. It occurred to me to take a picture. Or even better, a video. But the quality would be low using my crappy phone. Kirby's had a better camera... My own thoughts made me grin.

"Kitten, we should definitely do more porn together."

"I created a monster."

"Nah. You just set it free."

He laughed, burying his face into the cushions. I dragged my tongue through his crease, tasting our combined pleasure, then I tapped his ass cheek.

"Shower. C'mon."

We were supposed to meet Burke, Emerson, and Richard and his partner for dinner, and we couldn't go reeking of a two-hour fucking session.

KIRBY ACTED weird while we were getting ready. I was worried it had to do with the finished film. Maybe there was something I'd missed that he didn't like. But when I asked him, he insisted everything was fine.

In the cab on the way to the pub, Kirby pulled out a black sleep mask.

"Can you put this on?"

"What? We're meeting friends, kitten. I don't think it's appropriate to—"

"Oh, shut up and put it on."

Curious, I obeyed. "It's not my birthday yet."

"Your birthday is in May, I know. Be quiet and trust me."

At first, I tried to follow the car's movement to guess where we were going. It seemed we were headed to Burke's, but then I got lost. When Kirby dragged me out of the cab by my hand, I had to admit I had no idea where we were. The street sounded busy and smelled of gasoline with a hint of urine and cigarette smoke, so it must have been still in the city center, on the shabbier side. Maybe the bar district?

I stumbled, and Kirby muttered an apology.

"Almost there," he said.

A door creaked, and Kirby instructed me to step over something.

Then he pulled down the mask.

I blinked. Blinked again.

We stood in front of an open, red-painted door with a swirly "welcome" sign on the glass. I looked up the facade, then at Kirby's nervous expression, then back at the building in front of me.

"That's the old cocktail bar."

"Yes."

"Did they open again?"

"Not yet. But you will."

You will. Through the door, I could hear quiet instrumental music. A piece of paper was taped outside on the window glass, saying "Closed for private event."

"Me?" The puzzle pieces were slowly falling into place, but too many were still missing. "What the hell did you do?"

Hooking his arm through mine, Kirby led me inside where Richard stood all suited up, leaning on the bar counter. His boyfriend, Carter, sat behind him on a bar stool with a glass of champagne in his hand.

"Richard and I made a deal with Burke," Kirby said before I could properly greet them. "We're investing together so you two can branch out. Burke wants you to lead the new location if you're up for it."

I whirled around to face him. "You bought this bar?"

Kirby shrugged. "I got some more money from another

campaign I did in the fall, so I asked my adviser what to do with the cash. And then I called Richard."

"You got me a bar." He was unreal.

Grinning, Kirby nodded. "You like it?"

I opened my mouth and closed it a few times, no words forthcoming. Kirby grabbed my elbow and tugged me deeper into the room. I gazed around, not entirely sure I was awake. Did we take a nap after the sex? The alarm would surely beep any second now.

"This isn't real, is it?"

I yelped when Kirby pinched my arm. I guessed it was real, then.

"I think it looks nice, right?" he asked, a little unsure.

"It's beautiful, kitten. I don't know what to say."

The paneling seemed to be from before the recession, and even though it had been treated roughly, it wouldn't need much to restore it to its former glory. The booths had faux leather seats, cracked in the corners, and the floor had missing tiles. The green lamps must have been original or really good replicas. We'd need to rebuild the shelves behind the bar, the stools needed reupholstering, but the counter itself was in great condition. I smoothed my hand over the solid wood.

"We had a few contractors over already," Richard said from behind me. "We could sit down next week, you and I, and go through the offers. We've checked the plumbing and electrical work, and it's all good. The guy who ran this place before they made it into a restaurant must have taken good care of it. The kitchen requires a lot of work, but it's all safely within our budget."

I wasn't really in a state to take in all the information.

"You're in?" Burke's voice came from behind me, and I whirled around to see him by the door, holding little Bo to his chest. Emerson sat in one of the booths, grinning at me, Jay next to him with Monty under his arm, playing a game on his phone.

"Yeah," I breathed. "Sure. I'm in."

"So it was a good idea?" Kirby asked.

My head spinning, I found his nervous face. He looked a little blurry suddenly. I grabbed him and pulled him to me, my chest tight and eyes burning.

"I love you," I managed in a broken voice.

He hugged me back. "Happy?" he mumbled into my shirt.

"So happy. Thank you, love. Thank you so much."

"Someone give my bartender a drink, please," Burke said loudly, making everyone laugh.

Kirby had to disentangle himself because I would have mauled him in front of everyone. Carter handed me a glass, which I downed, so he poured me another.

When Richard guided me through the place, talking figures and renovation schedules, it all began sinking in. Burke and I would branch out with Kirby and Richard as investors. The plan was that if the bar did well, we would gradually buy them out. I would end up co-owning it with Burke. I was too keyed up to follow everything, but the numbers seemed incredibly generous. Apparently, Richard had been pushing Burke to expand for years, but Burke never had the drive for it. Now he was happy to branch out since I would be taking responsibility for the new location.

Within six months, we could be open.

Jay and Monty had to go home soon since it was a school night, but the rest of us stayed. After Emerson fed him, Bo fell asleep in his stroller, and we sat down in a booth, the six of us sharing a pizza delivery. I was surprised by how easy-going Richard seemed up close and personal. I carried a hefty load of prejudice against rich people, but Richard Porter would be my exception. I was excited to work with him.

Kirby sat cuddled under my arm, and Emerson eyed us with a shit-eating grin.

"I tried to bet Burke after our wedding that you would end up together. But I couldn't because he agreed with me."

"Except it took you two years longer than we thought," Burke said.

"I take the blame," Kirby said in a serious tone. "Hugh's the most patient guy on the planet."

"I'm not. You were just worth the wait." Squeezing him, I kissed his cheek. "I would have waited for however long you needed, kitten," I added into his ear.

Carter, who sat opposite Kirby, smiled wide, probably overhearing.

"So when's the movie coming?" Emerson asked.

Burke grimaced, shaking his head vehemently. "No. Please, no," he cried before Kirby or I could answer. "I'm sure it's great and all, but I'd like to be able to talk to you again."

Emerson agreed loudly he would never watch Kirby's films because that would be weird, but Richard seemed to be engrossed with his wine glass. I remembered him chatting to Kirby when they first met and realizing where he'd known him from. That had been fun. Carter was blushing a little, a small secretive smile on his lips. Did they watch porn together? Good for them. I figured they would surely have enough sense not to talk to us about it if they ever saw ours.

"We actually saw the final cut today. It was fun." Kirby sounded noncommittal, but under the table, he caressed my inner thigh. The little demon. We'd be watching it again, soon.

For me, the evening passed in an excited daze. I was still buzzing from the high while we waited for the cab home.

Kirby went home with me since I'd be taking Monty to school in the morning. We wanted to walk for a bit, so we let the cab drop us off a few blocks away from my apartment.

Something occurred to me as we strolled through the quiet street. "When did you decide to do this?" I asked.

Kirby hesitated. "I called Richard around the beginning of November."

"But that was before..." I trailed off, speechless once more.

He exhaled. "I knew you and Jay were struggling, and I figured this could help long term. You said you felt weird talking to Burke and Richard about it, but I could do it. They thought it was a good idea, so we began checking out the location, and Richard engaged a lawyer and a contractor. He was worried about hidden flaws in the building and some legal requirements or licenses or something like that. I didn't quite understand that stuff. But it all worked out great. Then you and I got together, and I was afraid it would be even weirder, but since Burke was on board..." Shrugging, he trailed off.

"I still can't believe you did that, Kirby."

"Why? It was something you wanted a lot, right? And I could give it to you. Of course I did it." He sounded like it was an everyday thing, people buying bars for each other. "And I didn't buy you a bar. I just invested in one, right?"

"It's a huge amount of money, kitten." After the exhilarating evening, the doubts were creeping in. What if I couldn't pull it off? What if the bar would be a flop?

"Richard told me the same thing. For him, it didn't matter at all because he's like a bazillionaire, so the bar is small change for him, but he thought I was taking a financial risk."

"You are. He's right, Kirby."

"Nah. He's dead wrong." Kirby slowed down and looked at me seriously. "If it doesn't work, at least we've tried, right? And it's just extra money. I don't need it." He laughed, spreading his arms wide. "I've got food, a great place, nice clothes, and when I turn the faucet, warm water comes out. And I could make you happy. I'm fucking lucky."

"You were making me happy already," I reminded him.

"If the bar does well, and the movie is a hit, then you and Jay can pay off the debt. We could buy a house in a nice neighborhood so Monty could go to a better school. We could fix it up so it would have two apartments—"

I blinked. "You want to live with us?"

Kirby's cheeks flushed, and he looked down, shrinking a bit. "Um. I don't want to put Jay in a weird position. Just because he's okay with me around Monty on weekends... I don't want to be like a bad influence. But maybe if the house had two units..."

Swallowing the lump in my throat, I hugged Kirby, tucking his head to my chest. "Kitten, Jay loves you. He doesn't think you are a bad influence or anything like that. He thinks you're great with Monty."

"No parent wants a former prostitute raising their kid."

"Actually, you'll be a fantastic influence. One day, Monty will understand why you didn't know anything about Legos and that the things he takes for granted can be rare treasures for others. He'll learn that the world isn't black and white. He'll learn about compassion and what harm prejudice does. And when he's old enough to properly talk about sex with you, he'll learn about consent and pleasure and love. Why would any of that be a bad influence?"

Leaning back, Kirby looked up at me with watery eyes. One corner of his mouth lifted. "Sweet talker," he said, his voice shaky. "You're just saying that because I got you a bar."

Laughing, I clutched him to me. "Kitten, I love you to death."

KIRBY

Eight months later

The promo tour for our summer project was over, and we'd been insanely busy with the cocktail bar, but our agent and Brian still booked us for at least one event a month. Cons, club openings, galas, product launches—we'd survived it all. Hugh was surprisingly unfazed, treating the crowds with the same decisive calm he used to approach drunks at the pub, and having him with me helped me to stay chill as well.

Tonight had been an award ceremony—we'd received a weird-ass abstract golden statue for the hottest couple in the industry, thank you very much—and now we were at the afterparty in a newly opened upper-class club downtown.

My man looked fabulous. Hugh in tight designer jeans, heavy boots, and an open vest revealing his magnificent chest was every omega's wet dream. His beard was neatly trimmed, head freshly shaved, and I couldn't stop running my fingers over his smooth scalp. He winked at me, grinning, and hauled me closer on the red sofa. When I was plastered to him, he put a possessive hand on my hip and nodded at the reporter. The club was buzzing, but here in the chill-out area, the music was low. Security stood at the entrance, keeping us separated from the throngs of people.

"What about your next heat, Kirby? Have you changed your mind? Are you filming with Hugh again?"

I looked at my man, biting my lip. "Nope. It'll be just us."

"Undisclosed location." Hugh smiled at me, his eyes warm.

"Meaning I have no idea where we'll be going," I said.

The reporter laughed. "But you have another upcoming project together, don't you?"

This time, it was Hugh who spoke. "We do. The post-production is almost finished. I'm not allowed to say much about it, only that it's different from anything Kirby has done before. The release party is next month."

The reporter's eyebrows flew up. "Different, you say. Dare we hope to see Kirby Matthews doing kink?"

It would be kinky all right. I still got hot and bothered remembering some of the scenes we'd done. But I made a zip gesture over my lips, and Hugh shrugged noncommittally. I was wearing cuffs on my wrists and a collar around my neck, which was entirely intentional. Our agent wanted us to build up the hype about our next film, and our outfits were chosen to drop the right hints. The silver chain led from my collar to Hugh's hand, and he tugged on it, so I leaned in and kissed him. Cameras flashed all around us.

"And what can you tell me about your contribution to the midnight auction here?"

"Oh hell." I hid my face in Hugh's neck. It had been his ridiculous idea. "You answer this one."

"We're auctioning off the sheer top Kirby wore on set of our heat film"—he paused, making a circle on my ass with his palm—"and his lace briefs from the same project."

The reporter all but squealed. "Oh my God, really?"

"The money goes directly to the Massoud charity, to a protected home for homeless omegas in heat. So I thought we'd better offer something worth a fat check."

"That's brilliant. It's going to be the climax of this event, I'm sure." He chuckled at his double meaning, and I repressed a sigh. "Rumor has it you've purchased a home together. Is it true?"

"We do live together, yes." Evasion was the key. Neither of us wanted to reveal our current living arrangements because of Jay and Monty, who lived in the eastern part of the two-story house. They had their own entrance, kitchen, two bedrooms, plus a big family bathroom, but we shared the garage, garden, and pool house. We'd managed to hide the address from public records, and the longer it remained a secret, the better.

"Kirby, the collar you're wearing. Is that simply an accessory, or does it have a deeper meaning?"

Hugh tugged on it again, and I grinned. "Means I'm taken."

"Hugh, you've been dubbed on social media as the luckiest alpha in Dalton City. What do you think about that?"

"It's true," Hugh said, deadpan.

"Are you exclusive, or will you be working with other performers eventually?"

"We're exclusive." My answer was quick and clear. We kept getting the same question over and over, and it was beginning to annoy me. I had zero interest in doing anything with anyone else but my mate. In fact, my skin crawled at the thought.

Hugh patted my hip, sensing my discomfort. "We have to wrap up," he said. "Kirby needs something to drink before we have to be on stage for the auction."

The reporter gave him a polite smile. "Of course. Thank you so much for your time."

My man led me through the chill-out area to the bar with his arm around my back and the silver chain from my collar in his hand. The crowd parted, and more cameras flashed. I was good at ignoring them now and almost never winced. It helped that with Hugh by my side, people gave me space almost instinctively.

Hugh brushed my lower back, tracing the lace that peeked above my low-cut pants. He nuzzled my temple when we waited for our drinks.

"New?" he whispered into my ear.

"Uh-huh."

"Can't wait to see you in them."

He pushed one finger into my underwear, teasing the top of my crease just for a second.

I imagined myself on my knees later tonight. I'd suck him off in front of the mirror so he could watch my ass encased in the sheer black material while he came down my throat. I leaned into him, hiding my face in his chest. His scent enveloped me, so safe and familiar.

"Are you tired, kitten?"

"Not tired, but I want to go home early."

"I'll text Brian we're leaving right after the auction."

"Thanks."

I lifted his hand to my lips and kissed his knuckles.

The luckiest alpha in the city. Little did they know I was the lucky one.

ABOUT THE AUTHOR

Queer fiction author Roe Horvat was born in the former Czechoslovakia which equipped him with a dark sense of sarcasm and a penchant for good beer. Roe traveled Europe and finally settled in Sweden. He came out as transgender in 2017 and has been fabulous since. He loves Jane Austen, Douglas Adams, bad action movies, stand-up comedy, the great Swedish outdoors, and all kinds of earthly pleasures. When not hiding in the studio doing graphics, he can be found trolling cafés and pubs in Gothenburg, writing.

Website: roehorvat.com

ALSO BY ROE HORVAT

.